Hondon Writers Circle

STORY TELLING TWENTY SEVEN

My appreciation to HondonVillas SL for sponsoring this booklet.
"""""

Also grateful thanks on behalf of the Writers Circle for the help given by Senor Victor Ramirez Segura, at the Ayuntamiento
"""""

The Asociación de Vecinos de Hondón de los Frailes

We are thankful to the The Residents' Association and their President for the history and details of the proposed over development of the village which was removed through their efforts.

The Association is administered by a committee who are selected by the residents at its AGM and is a legal entity registered in Valencia in 2006 with a set of Statutes to govern its operation.

On page 9 we tell the story of its foundation and its achievements by its President Philip Woolford.

Contacts: presidente@frailesvecinos.es or vicepresidenta@frailesvecinos.es

I0520192

Hondon Writers Circle

STORY TELLING TWENTY SEVEN

The

Hondon Writers

Circle

'Story Telling 27' was assembled and
produced in Hondon de los Frailes
in the delightful Hondon Valley, Spain
by Percychatteybooks.

The Hondon Valley consists of small picturesque villages in South East, Spain, set in the mountains and nestling in amongst the agricultural fields of grape vines, almond trees and other greenery with the birds singing and the occasional sound of a tractor.

The Hondon Writers Circle comprises a group of people from many different walks of life working as individuals to write, compare and improve their writing skills.

THIS BOOKLET INCLUDES STORIES NOT TOLD BEFORE AND WRITTEN BY MEMBERS OF THE HONDON WRITERS CIRCLE ALL ARE UNIQUE AND DIFFERENT, IT ALSO INCLUDES TRAILERS FROM PUBLISHED BOOKS.

STORY TELLING HAS ITEMS
TO MAKE YOUR DAY
VIA POEMS, FUNNIES AND
THINGS TO SAY.
WORDS TO MOVE YOU,
OTHERS TO PLEASE
THEN THERE ARE THOSE
WHO ARE THERE TO TEASE.
THERE ARE LONG ONES,
INTERESTING ONES TOO.
SOME ARE MISCHIEVOUS
BUT NEVER BLUE,
ALL IN ALL A BOOKLET
TO HOLD AND IS TRUE.

To my wife Jean, my love and soul mate, I am ever grateful for the help and support in developing this and other work. Percy

Hondon Writers Circle

STORY TELLING TWENTY SEVEN

ISBN 978 1 9162712 1 0

Published by: Percychatteybooks Publisher

© Percy W Chattey 2019

 **Hello! I am Meg and I will be your host throughout, with descriptions where they are needed.**

Our grateful thanks to
Derek Cook for the cover

Also Members of the Writers Circle who have written articles in this book

Richard Seal
Sarah Dawkins RN, BSc (Hons) MSc
Trudie Le Beau
Caroline Goss
S J Tarsus
Percy Chattey
Karen Kopczynska
Debbie Freeman
Tarika Gradva
Lin Penhaul
and Meg for hosting

The Hondon Writers Circle, whose members between meetings, write narratives on a given subject hence we have printed stories with similar headings.

THE FOLLOWING ARTICLE WAS COMMISSIONED FOR AND FIRST PUBLISHED IN THE 2018 HONDON DE LOS FRAILES 'FIESTA BROCHURE'

The Hondon Valley

Percy Chattey

This refuge! This quiet sanctuary away from the pace, hassle and bustle which is the world beyond the shelter of the Hondon Valley. This beautiful Spanish neighbourhood nestling in between the mountains less than one hour's drive from the golden beaches of the Costa Blanca coast.

It is a region which can trace its roots back to Roman Times, the stone terracing still surviving, although unused and overgrown on the mountain side give presence to that period. The small stone huts dotted around the landscape shows evidence of a later time, when men toiled

the fields and these ancient and time worn constructions were places to rest from their labour, or they were for the shepherd to shelter and to take a break whilst looking after the flock.

This valley, this refuge from the madness of the outside world, is where the quiet relaxed pace of time is paramount to everyday living. The mixture of different people mainly north Europeans who have found the delights of this place in the clean air of the mountains making it their home, mixing in as one, creating a contented community with its self-governing bodies controlling the smooth running of events. The street parties and the ·fiesta in July and August ... not to be missed as people come from far and wide to see the spectacles and to enjoy the cuisine offered by its restaurants.

From their humble beginnings the two communities of the valley with their grand old Churches to the centre of each built and named by the Dominican Friars so long a time ago. As the bells of the churches mark each hour the surroundings progress into the new age well equipped to welcome all who wish to live or holiday in its peaceful environment.

A tale of...
The Residents' Association

The Asociación de Vecinos de Hondón de los Frailes

Once upon a time there was a sleepy village of some 600 souls nestling in a valley between the Sierra Crevillente and the Sierra de los Frailes and growing slowly as people discovered this peaceful community... then a big, bad developer came along and said "let me spoil your idyll with 5,000 houses and a golf course and I will give your community the crumbs that fall from my table". Thus, was born the 2005 Plan General. Then came together a great gathering of the villagers who with one voice cried this shall not pass... and from this gathering emerged 7 valiant people who devised a cunning plan... they would organise a group of neighbours (Vecinos) to undertake opposition to the plan. And from this start emerged a group of volunteers who became The Asociación de Vecinos de Hondón de los Frailes, a legal entity registered in Valencia in 2006 and with a set of Statutes to govern its operation.

Money was needed to pay for legal advice, travel expenses and such things, so the members made significant contributions over several years and a fighting fund was established to enable the collective voice of the community to be heard. The development of the 2005 Plan General was slowed and eventually was cancelled by the Valencian Government. So, a Dragon was slain...!

Not a lot later, another Dragon stalked the valley... a bypass road was proposed that was poorly designed and which would have cut off more than 300 residents in the campo from the village. Members of the committee again exercised the right to represent the membership to government and travelled to Valencia where they met with the road designers and secured many changes to the design. This activity continued until an even bigger Dragon called 'Financial Crisis' stalked the land and killed off the project.

There hasn't been much fighting since that, only with a Dragonette, but there isn't a concrete factory at the upwind edge of the village! Then Brexit happened, or didn't, and much effort has been deployed on keeping the large contingent of British expats in the community informed about process and effect. At the same time, the new Plan General was developed, the relevant parts translated into English and the membership kept informed, and it was accepted with hardly a murmur.

Soon, a new focus will be needed and new blood required to sustain the association so that it remains available to use its statutory power of representation should circumstances change and another Dragon stalks the land. The statutes limit activities to non-profit making and for the benefit of the community, similarly membership is restricted to people who are resident, full or part time, in the village. Within those bounds almost anything is possible.

Some members of the committee have served in one role or another for 7 years and it is time to step aside. If you live in the community and are not a member, please consider joining the association. If you can contribute to running the Association, please consider standing for election at our AGM in February.

Contacts: presidente@frailesvecinos.es or
vicepresidenta@frailesvecinos.es

This is a lovely story from Trudie, who is a prolific writer and has had three books published which are written about times of old. She writes regularly for the Writers Circle

Josh's Dilemma

Trudie Le Beau

Sergeant Josh McGiven sat at his desk regretting the late work night and the one too many whiskies he'd downed in an effort to get a decent nights ' sleep. Life hadn't been going too well over the last year, what with Carol hounding him for more child allowance and being overlooked for the promotion that he thought was in the bag, and now he was being pressured to find the perpetrator of a series of seemingly aimless murders which had them all baffled and which was putting his unit under rather unfavourable scrutiny. No one had said anything thus far but Josh and his team were well aware that their failing efforts were being closely monitored.

He took the files that he'd left on his desk the night before and spread them out. He picked up the file of the first victim and decided to start at the beginning and re-interview their one and only witness. He saw that she was a Mrs Whitlock and he noticed that she lived just two streets away from his rented flat. He pondered on the details – an elderly woman who had found the victim after deciding to investigate two loud bangs that she had heard nearby. As she'd approached the victim, she had seen someone running away but her eyes were not good enough to make out any details, other than she assumed it to be a man and he seemed to move rapidly. When asked she thought his clothing to be dark coloured.

Josh made his way to his car with the file under his arm which also contained pictures of the subsequent five victims – you never knew. Mrs Whitlock lived in a quiet leafy road on the outskirts of town in just the kind of house he and Carol always said they wanted to end up in – but that was a life time ago. He rang the bell which gave rise to a dog barking somewhere at the back of the house, and after a few minutes the door opened a few inches and the face of a very diminutive elderly lady peered out.

"Good morning madam. I'm Detective Sergeant McGiven and I wondered if I could just take a minute of your time."

Ada's heart began to thump, and she hoped the young man didn't hear the quake in her voice as she asked for identity. He seemed more than happy to oblige and actually congratulated her on being so careful. She opened the door to admit him and called out to Bobby to be quiet.

Josh was shown into what Mrs Whitlock liked to call the lounge and explained that as they were not making any headway in these killings, he had decided to review every case once more in the hope that something might turn up. He accepted the offer of tea, glad of the opportunity to exercise his policeman's curiosity and have a look round. He noticed a photograph of a middle-aged couple both dressed in army uniform that took pride of place on the mantelpiece. So, Mrs Whitlock was ex-army – who would have thought.

Ada busied herself making tea. She told herself to breathe deeply as her mind raced. What did this man want? What did he know? She put the teapot, cups and saucers and plate of biscuits on a tray and, trying to sound as jolly as she could she spoke to Bobby, "Come on Bobby we've got a visitor – come in and meet the nice man."

Josh thought Ada, as she insisted upon being called, to be absolutely charming, and her little dog Bobby was just the kind of companion he would like. Never mind, back to business. He opened the file and read out Ada's statement asking her to think hard, could she remember anything else at all that she had left out. Ada sat, pretending to concentrate, "Well, only that I knew they were gun shots. I'm ex-army you see so I knew the sound. Not that I used firearms of course, Stan – that's my husband – we were in admin – logistics and that sort of thing." Ada looked wistful, "I do miss him so – that's why I got Bobby, so I wouldn't be on my own".

Josh was reluctant to submit Ada to any more upset, but he had a job to do so he asked her to study the faces of all the victims – it was a long shot but she might possibly know one or more of them. Ada didn't have to feign being upset – the last thing she ever wanted to do was see again the faces of the men she had killed, she took out her hankie and blew her nose. "Oh, those poor men, and so many of them but I'm afraid no, I've never seen any of them before – who were they; were they gangsters?"

Josh had to smile at the old-fashioned terminology "I can't say too much Mrs Whitlock, but thank you for your time anyway, and for the refreshments."

Ada waved to her visitor as he pulled away from her house then went inside to pour a large glass of port. "Oh Bobby, that was a frightener, and no mistake."

When Josh returned to the office there was a note confirming that the gun used to kill victim number six was the same as that used on all other five.

Over the next few days Josh re-interviewed the families of the first five victims and with the passing of time and less fear of incriminating themselves some of them spoke more freely, admitting that not all the deaths had exactly been bad news. Slowly but surely Josh was able to establish that these men had been guilty of extreme domestic violence and having seen the partner of victim number six he had no doubts that he fell into the same category. So there was a connection and maybe a motive but what linked these families to the killer. He doubted that any of them would have the money or the nous to take out a contract – or was it one of them? He would just have to keep on digging.

It was a couple of weeks before he got around once again to visiting Julie Forbes. In truth he had been putting off visiting Shedwell. It was a miserable place and he was always worried about the condition his car would be in if it was left for more than ten minutes. He noticed how much better she was looking than the first time he'd interviewed her. The flat was clean and tidy, and she had definitely put on a bit of weight which suited her – she was actually a very pretty girl. As he had done with all the others, he laid out the photos of all the victims but once more he drew a blank, Julie did not recognise anyone.

He pulled out of the estate thankful that his car was still intact, slowing down to allow an elderly woman and her pooch cross the road.   Mrs Whitlock was buttoned up against the chill wind, but it was Bobby that he recognised. He lowered his window, "Mrs Whitlock, what a surprise, I wouldn't have expected to see you in this area."

Ada looked up recognising him immediately and waved, but he was sure he saw a glimpse of annoyance – or was it fear in the split second before she had composed herself. "Oh, Bobby and I have just been for our afternoon walk." She pointed toward the open land beyond, "We just come here occasionally – it makes a change and Bobby loves to play with other dogs." She smiled "I suppose I could say the same about you – I don't think policemen are particularly popular around here do you?"

"Just following up on a lead; do you know anyone in Shedwell?"

"Not that I'm aware of. I think some of the dog walkers may live here or here about, but we never do more than just pass the time of day."

"Can I give you a lift?"

"That is very kind of you sergeant but my car is parked just down the road so we are fine," she looked down at her dog, "Aren't we Bobby."

Josh wished her well and continued on his way. Something had ignited his interest. It was a coincidence seeing Ada here today, and he never did like coincidences. As he drove along he told himself not to be so stupid. The case was getting to him and he was clutching at straws. By the time he reached his office he had managed to convince himself that he must be losing the plot.

He sat at his desk frowning. There was something floating around in his brain but it just wouldn't come to the fore. His hand hovered over the files that were still spread on his desk and he picked up file number two. He leafed through the pages almost trying to divine a clue and then he saw it. The words jumped out at him, the bullets were from a handgun, maybe a Beretta, and someone had scrawled in the margin *ex-military*? He remembered the photograph on Ada's mantelpiece – another coincidence.

On a whim he decided to check up on something and within half an hour he was back knocking on the door of Julie Forbes. After assuring her that she was not in any trouble he asked her to go over her movements from a week or so prior to the murder of her partner. Julie gradually relaxed and began to describe her pretty humdrum existence which was regularly interspersed with beatings that she was thankful she no longer had to suffer. Josh asked if anything out of the ordinary had happened – anything no matter how small and seemingly insignificant.

"Well there was one time." Josh sat up, all ears.

"It was when Gary was really laying in to me. We'd well – you know, just been to bed and I was getting dressed when he started accusing me of having other men in here when he wasn't around. It was stupid of course, but he'd worked himself up into a real temper. He punched me a few times and I was really scared so I just grabbed my coat and ran outside. I didn't think what I was doing, and I just ran," she hesitated.

"Go on Julie, nothing you say will get you into any kind of trouble."

"Well I just ran and because my eye had swollen, and I suppose I was crying, I just bumped into this lady – nearly knocked her over." Josh could feel the hairs on his neck bristling.

"She was a lovely old girl. Made me get into her car and covered me up with her dog's blanket. She was really kind."

"Then what happened?"

"I saw Gary coming after me, so I scooted. Didn't want to get her into trouble – he could be really nasty, and he didn't care who to. We went back indoors and of course he was lovely then, promised he wouldn't touch me ever again," she shrugged, "Some hopes."

Josh was just about to speak when Julie carried on.

"Wasn't long before he stamped on my hand and split my lip because little Eddie was crying. I don't mind telling you I was at the end of my tether by then. Anyway, I saw the old girl again when I was out shopping. I could tell she felt sorry for me. She wanted to buy me a drink and have a chat, and she was so kind and understanding that I was on the verge of asking her for help, but I saw Gary outside in the car park drumming his fingers on the steering wheel and I lost my nerve." She looked at Josh defiantly, "It's good to know there are some nice people in the world anyway."

"You say this lady had a dog; I don't suppose you know her name."

"No, but she was lovely and so was her little dog, Bobby his name was."

It was a little time later when,

Josh's head was spinning as he drove toward Ada's house. All roads lead to Ada, but that was crazy. He was sure now that she was involved somehow, but how? Did she have an accomplice? Was she paying someone to kill these men, and if so why? Admittedly the world was a better place without them – in his opinion at least, but how were all these deaths connected? Were they being eliminated because of what they were?

Once more he heard Bobby barking when he rang the doorbell and once more Ada opened the door just a few inches and this time Josh noticed that she had put on the safety chain. "Oh! Mr McGiven; how nice to see you again." She took off the chain and let him in, "You can't be too careful with all these murders going on. Do come in and I'll make some tea and I've some freshly baked scones; now how can I help?"

The house smelled deliciously of baking and Josh was shown into the lounge. He'd brought along the same photos of the deceased men as before, but this time he'd added a few lines of description to them as he'd noticed previously that she didn't seem to bother with glasses which didn't quite tally with the poor eyesight alluded to in her witness statement.

He watched Ada carry the tray laden with tea, scones, butter and jam and realised that he'd made the common mistake of underestimating her just because she was elderly. Yes, she had white hair and was in her seventies, but her movements were swift and agile, almost athletic. Her mind was sharp and clear and now that he thought about it, her years in the army were evident in that everything about her home and herself was orderly and ship shape.

He spread the pictures out for her to peruse which she did, picking up each one and reading aloud the text that he had introduced – without the aid of spectacles. "Your eyesight is better than mine Ada, I couldn't do that without having my lenses in – or do you have lenses too."

He saw it then. She didn't alter her expression, but he knew she was on to him. "Not for reading no, but I'm not so hot at distances." They both knew her answer was a little lame.

"These scones are delicious Ada. You'll have to give me the recipe – I live on my own now and I must be the world's worst cook." He quickly changed tack, "Do you own a gun at all? I mean, I know it isn't legal, but I just wondered, with you and your husband being in the military." His words hung in the air.

Ada finished the mouth full of scone and smiled with her mouth only, "Why on earth would I have a gun and how would I get one? We were both in the military, but it's strictly forbidden to….."

"Yes of course," he shook his head, "It was a silly thing to say."

This was surreal. Here he was eating home-made buttered scones and drinking tea with a would-be serial murderer. He took a sip from his cup – how to approach this.

The nice sergeant was obviously preoccupied, and Ada sensed the game was up. "Tell me sergeant, if you caught this killer I suppose they would face a life in jail and…."

"For murdering six men – I should certainly think so. Whoever is guilty would spend the rest of their life locked up with absolutely no chance of release."

"Do you think you will ever catch him?"

Josh chose his words carefully "Well we have a lot of leads that don't quite tie up, but we are piecing the jigsaw together and of course he, or she, will make a mistake eventually, they always do."

"So, reading between the lines, you seem to be saying that if there were no more occurrences these murders will remain unsolved."

"That's about it in a nutshell."

"You already know the truth don't you sergeant?" Josh choked and began to cough. He had not expected this. "Oh, it's alright. I would never harm you. It was just all those poor women you see," she dug her nails into the palms of her hands, "Those dreadful cruel men just did as they pleased, and no-one was there to help – I felt it was my duty do you see? There, I've admitted it to you but of course I'll deny ever having done so." Ada picked up the tray and spoke as a matter of fact, "Just thought it would be good to clear the air sergeant McGiven.

Now, I'll make a fresh pot of tea, and would you like another scone?

Josh was too shocked to formulate any words, so just shook his head to the affirmative.

Josh, still a little dazed climbed into his car carrying the file of photos and a recipe for Ada's fruit scones. What the hell was he going to do? He'd just spent an hour with a most unlikely murderer and he had no proof other than her admission. There were no witnesses, no gun, nothing to tie her directly to all six crimes, and the worst thing was that he had grown quite fond of the old girl. By the time he reached his office, and after a great deal of soul searching, he had decided to keep her secret and just back peddle with his investigations, after all, doing much else would just be a complete waste of police time and public money.

Ada rinsed out the teapot and washed up the tea plates and butter knife. "Well Bobby, it's in the lap of the Gods now. First thing tomorrow we'll take a little trip out to get rid of the gun and then we'll just have to wait and see what the good sergeant does." She bent to ruffle the dog's head, "Right my lad, we'd better get you out for your walk before the light fails."

As they strolled along to the local park Ada was deep in thought. "Well Bobby, you know I like to have a project on the go, but we can't carry on with my old one now we've been found out, so I think I'll concentrate on finding sergeant McGiven a partner; the poor man must be lonely," she thought for a moment then reached a decision, "That Julie was a nice girl – maybe they would both like to come round for lunch one day. Yes, I think that would be a good place to start."

Bobby didn't quite understand what his mistress was saying, but he sensed her good mood and they were going to the park, so as far as he was concerned all was well in the world.

\\\\\\\\

A group of lovely words and a thought-provoking piece by Janne Tarika Gravdal

Your Soul and Your Spirit

are truly You

Your Thoughts are Your Future

They were also Your past

So dream on, be happy

See yourself wonderfully free

for you are still the master

of your faith,

you are still the captain of your soul

Introducing Caroline with a fictional tale of how Government in Westminster performs ... her articles are always interesting, full of detail with an agreeable story line.

Speaker -

The 'Maiden' Speech

Caroline Goss

"Order, Order," the familiar command that everyone knew in the Houses of Parliament. The debate on Funding Childcare Facilities was heated between the two main political parties and she knew she had to take charge again of the situation as was her right as the Speaker of the House of Commons.

****

Ten years ago her written nomination was submitted to the Commons Table Office at nine thirty on the morning of the election. She put herself forward as a contender as procedure dictates and at two thirty that afternoon she addressed the House.

The Right Honourable and Honourable Members of the Palace of Westminster were seated in the traditional green leather benches tiered on either side by men in dull black and grey suits, colourful shirts and bright bold ties and women in bright coloured designer suits and carefully coiffed hair much as it was today.

The debate to choose another Speaker for the House had begun and was again the normal electrically charged banter cascading from side to side of the House. The front benchers wiled their charms with their euphoric speeches and engaged with the lesser known backbenchers who were enjoying the ping pong of political debate amongst cheers and jeers as speeches were made to support those MP's to take on the non-judgmental role of Speaker.

To be Speaker of the House she knew Parliamentary Constitution would place a unique position on her and although a lonely post without the camaraderie of her party she knew being impartial was an essential requisite of the job.

She felt confident enough that she would pass the hurdles of democracy, she began working for several weeks on her maiden speech making sure it was perfect, scrutinising every word and even talking out loud in front of her mirror. Being the first woman Speaker would indeed be a huge privilege; she wanted the job to be of her own merits of wisdom, charisma and confidence and not sentiment or equality because she is a woman.

Over an hour of credible and sometimes overzealous statement of political and historical points the

Presiding member asked Members of the House to make their votes. This was a secret ballot where each member had one vote to choose one candidate out of the four members who were in the running. The first session was completed and there was no overall majority, her heart was thumping fast and furious but on the outside her calm and demure manner won her many admirers in the political arena. She knew the candidate with the fewest votes would be eliminated, and when the vote was announced it wasn't her and another round of voting resumed. The members left the Chamber again to the Division Lobbies where they cast their secret vote and a while later returned; the Clerk came in the House with the results and handed them to the presiding member; she felt a pang of excitement and almost disbelief but held her head up high as her name was proposed and seconded and the Right Honourable Rebecca Elizabeth Merton was elected as the next Speaker of the House of Commons. She took the Chair as Speaker-elect or as was the custom 'dragged' to the Chair by her supporters. Standing proud and full of emotion with speech in her hand she commanded the audience of the distinguished members of the House as the silence drew them to her. She began, "In accordance to custom I now submit myself to the will of this House," she was in her element and the speech she had worked so hard on was soon discarded as she spoke sincerely from her heart. "I am honoured to take my place in this House. I would first like to pay tribute to our former Speaker the Right Honourable Bernard Legg. I know Speakers do not have friends, but he was my friend as I wish all of you to be," she raised her finger and in an arch like a car windscreen wiper swept it from right to left and back again as she said, "But I will favour none of you!" A great ruckus of laughter filled the house from both sides and from then on she knew they had accepted her.

She was in her element and continued with gusto, "I am with no doubt aware of the enormous importance and responsibility that is now placed on me as Speaker of this House. I am seen to be a just and fair person and essentially I have a sense of humour that I hope will not offend or anger anyone. I am as my Honourable friends have said previously, decisive, can make clear decisions and will stand by my decision in a fair but humoured way. Sometimes this House can be hard headed but don't feel complacent because I am a woman for, I will stop you in your tracks of any conduct that is not becoming of your position. Remember the Commons is my life and not just a career and being elected as Speaker of the House will be the greatest experience of my life and knowing I have your support I will conduct proceedings with the best of my ability for Queen and country".

She was sincere, she was honest, and she was unstoppable, "This position of Speaker bestowed upon me is the very embodiment of this historical constitution woven into the fabric of Parliament. I will discharge my responsibility to facilitate the legislature of the House of Commons to the best of my ability without fear or favour."

Her maiden speech continued for a good twenty minutes or so and the House was jubilant with excitement. The passion that she had roused in the honourable members emanated into a furore of hand clapping, 'hear, hear' , and the banging of tables and benches. She was moved but stood there elated, proudly soaking it all in.

****

That was ten years ago, and her time had almost come to retire from this eminent yet lonely position. She was the voice of the House and her duty to safeguard the rights and conduct of the proceedings of the House and its people had been an honour.

****

"Order, Order," her voice resounded across the halls of power. She pointed her finger at the honourable member; the Speaker had spoken, and the House began to silence into rumbling murmurs as the debate on Funding Childcare Facilities continued. It was nearing midnight and at an appropriate point in the proceedings she stood up and said "The House is to adjourn, say 'Aye' to adjourn," The house bellowed out 'Aye' in a long drawl and the Right Honourable Rebecca Elizabeth Merton stood up and said, "The Ayes's have it, the Ayes's have it".

""""""

The Plaza, Hondon de las Nieves

Story telling by Richard comes naturally with eight books published, and a ninth on the way, he writes from a wealth of experience. This is a charming tale of a young man trying to find his roots. However, the train trip across Australia did not go as he expected'

Cook

Richard Seal

Rick felt as if he had been travelling for most of his life. He had dropped out of Bath University in 1997, during his first year, having decided that the experience was not for him; the troubled teenager wanted to get away from everything and everyone for a while to re-energise and reflect on the future. A few months spent hitch-hiking around Europe turned into years, and he eventually ended up losing touch with his family. A fractious relationship with his parents and older brother contributed to the parting of the ways - there seemed to be little point in phoning or writing any more. The young man had no problems finding cash-in-hand work in bars, restaurants and shops and he tried to live as simply as possible in hostels, and even sleeping rough on occasion. By the time he found himself in Australia, in 2008, he had been away from his native England for over a decade.

The traveller had enjoyed his six month stay in Sydney; his job in a museum's post room had been congenial, and his workmates were very friendly - they did not hesitate in involving the 'Whinging Pom' in their banter. He spent several months living with his girlfriend in her flat, but things started to go awry when she lost her position as a medical secretary; the relationship broke down soon afterwards, and it felt like the right time for him to be on the move again. Rick decided to take the mammoth three-day trip on the Indian Pacific train from Australia's East to West Coast, and he was looking forward to spending the festive period in Fremantle or on one of Perth's lovely beaches. The man felt confident that he would be able to gate crash a party or a barbecue somewhere.

Having opted for the economy option for his rail trip, Rick quickly found himself shifting around in his seat, struggling to get comfortable, and suffering with intermittent cramp. By the time the train reached Orange East Fork Junction after six hours, his bottom was already feeling numb. If he had had any doubts at all that this would feel like a very long journey, they were quickly extinguished during the first night when a group of friends insisted on playing cards noisily throughout the small hours while a baby cried incessantly. The man had very little sleep and felt very groggy as dawn broke - he was suffering from the sensation of a heavy hangover without the benefit of having enjoyed any alcohol. Still, he managed to keep his sense of humour and made copious notes with a view to including the incident in a travel article at a later date.

The wonderful sounding Broken Hill, in the far west of outback New South Wales, was the first stop in the early morning. After eighteen hours the man was glad to have the chance to leave the train, grab a quick coffee to help to restore his sanity, and stretch his legs for twenty minutes or so. Back on board, he spent most of day two staring out of the window at the sparse desert scenery, trying in vain to spot a kangaroo. He was unable to settle to reading anything and made a point of avoiding eye contact with the tetchy-looking card school, who now seemed to be feeling somewhat worse for wear. The baby had not run out of his enthusiasm for crying, however, and remained in fine voice. The next chance for a break was at Adelaide station in the late afternoon, and it could not come soon enough for Rick.

Fortunately, the second night on the train proved to be more peaceful, as a lot of people, including the card players, had got off in Adelaide. The entire crew seemed to have changed at that stop too, whereas bleary-eyed passengers like him were hanging on in there for the duration. Rick managed to doze on and off and being either awake and asleep seemed to blur into a kind of dazed haze. The next stop, at 11.30 that morning, was Cook. He had read that it was a ghost town, with a population of four. When the place had been active, water was pumped up from underground but now it was carried in by train.

When the train arrived at Cook, Rick was immediately struck by its remoteness and the hand-painted sign warning "last fuel for 868 kilometres" He was intrigued to experience the atmosphere, having done some research on the place: It was created in 1917 when the railway was built, and had been a thriving community before World War II, but the decline seemed to begin with the switch from steam to diesel, then the downward spiral accelerated at the end of the 1990s with the privatisation of the railways. The bush hospital, which had advertised itself with "If you're crook, come to Cook", was no longer in operation, and there were now just a few houses and diesel refuelling facilities.

As he strolled around the tiny, deserted place Rick tried to imagine what it might have been like years before when there were around fifty inhabitants. Did children run around and play here? There was clearly a swimming pool at one time, but it was now filled in with dirt. There was no school, stores (except a gift shop which was only open when the train arrived) or sign of life, with nothing but desert to be seen in all directions. The silence was palpable. Deciding to sit in the secluded shade behind one of the deserted buildings, the man was entranced by the vision of indefinite nothingness. Enjoying the relief of being out of the punishing sunshine for a few moments, he became aware that his eyelids felt heavy ...

Awaking with a start, Rick found that the shade had moved around, and his lower legs were now in the direct sunlight. He hoped he had not got too burnt. It seemed even quieter now, and he could no longer hear the voices of fellow passengers, happy to have the chance for a short walk, but happier that they did not actually live in Cook. The man got up, returned to the dirt track, and almost fainted at what he saw: The train was gone. He stood motionless as he tried to come to terms with his situation. How on earth could it have left without him, he had only been asleep for a few minutes, surely? A glance at his watch revealed that he had actually been dead to the world for over two hours. Why would anyone think to check behind the broken-down shack? He checked his pockets, then remembered with horror that his phone was with his ticket and wallet inside his jacket, which, like all his other worldly possessions, still on the train and on route to Perth. He had a ten dollar note and his credit card on him, but nothing else.

He tried not to let panic set in, telling himself that it must be possible to talk to someone who could help him. The man remembered reading that one couple managed the servicing facilities for the Indian-Pacific, but when he got to the only house that looked vaguely lived-in, he found that it was locked up and in darkness. He called out, then walked up and down checking all the disused buildings to see if he could find any signs of life. Fortunately, he came across two large canisters of water, so he knew he would be able to survive. If he got desperate, he could always try breaking into the house. After sheltering in the shade again for a while, Rick walked alongside the railway line and discovered the town's long disused jail cells. The two very small corrugated iron sheds looked more like outhouses than anything else. As he emerged from the darkness within, he was shocked to find himself face to face with a rugged-looking man.

"G'day." Rick almost screamed with the shock. "Hello ... I'm sorry you gave me quite a fright there. My name's Rick."

"Ashley." The men shook hands.

"Do you live here, Ashley, there doesn't seem to be anyone around."

"Not exactly! Have you lost your train by any chance?"

"It left without me! I have no phone, everything has gone except the clothes that I'm wearing. I thought people were here to provide services for the train."

"Maybe they've gone away for a short break, the next train won't be in town for two or three days after all."

"Really?" He could feel anxiety starting to rise.

"The Indian-Pacific only runs once a week in each direction these days, funding cuts I suppose."

"Are there no other trains?"

"Well, for many years the inhospitable Nullarbor Plain was served by the Tea and Sugar Train which provided essential supplies to remote settlements."

"That's a relief, do you know when it's due?"

"The last train ran back in 1996, I believe. Tough break, mate."

Rick looked at the stranger, frowning. "Yes, I'm not too lucky today, am I?"

"I would agree with that. It's 100 kilometres to the south to reach the Eyre Highway, which crosses the Nullarbor, while both Adelaide and Perth are more than 1000 kilometres away on either side. It takes over five hours to get to Ceduna by car from here."

"Okay, I think you've cheered me up more than enough now, thanks. Why don't you tell me why you're here?"

"Well, the road from the highway to Cook isn't so great. I was driving down it alone late at night and broke down in the middle of nowhere. I couldn't get a phone signal and made the grave mistake of leaving the car and trying to walk to find help."

"Oh dear."

"What can I say? I know that it was a stupid decision. I was tired, disorientated and ended up wandering off into the desolate wilderness. You don't last too long out there without any food and water, especially with the heat of the day bearing down. It's highly unlikely that anyone will see you."

"How did you manage to make it to Cook on foot?"

The man looked at him with a blank expression. "I didn't ... "

Rick stared at him. "What do you mean? You're a ..."

"Ghost?" He chuckled. "I don't know about that. However, whatever you believe, it's true that my body perished and I've been stuck here, hanging around in a place that time has forgotten for way too long."

"I don't know what to say. Is there anything that I can do to help you?"

The man gave him a curious smile. "I'm glad you asked me that question. In actual fact, there is something you can do - let me use your body and you can stay here and take my place haunting Cook."

"What?" Ricky could not believe what he was hearing.

"Yes, it does sound a bit far fetched, doesn't it? I didn't think you'd be too keen on the idea, to be honest ... Nevertheless, it's my plan and I need to make the most of this opportunity. Another piece of bad luck for you, I'm afraid."

"Are you mad?" Ricky started backing away from Ashley.

"Possibly. I'm certainly very bored, and it's high time that I got the next train out of here."

"Look, I'm really sorry about what happened to you, but I still need my body as I happen to be living in it at the moment."

"That can soon be changed .. "

"Don't threaten me, you'd better stay away. I'm still alive, mate, and intend to stay that way. I'll be keeping an eye out for you."

"That's fine, relax. I'm in no rush, neither of us are going anywhere anytime soon. You'll have to go to sleep sometime, Rick, and I'll be ready to make my move."

Ricky felt frantic. He did not know where to go or what to say, he just knew he had to get away from the man and walked across to the opposite end of the street. There was no hiding place, no safe refuge, and the traveller soon started feeling weary. He knew it would be a huge battle to stay awake until the next train arrived ...

Two days later staff on the Indian Pacific were surprised to see a passenger request to join the train at the stop in Cook, South Australia. The quiet man paid for his ticket by credit card and took his seat in the economy carriage to begin his long journey back to Sydney. The young Englishman's train trip across Australia did not go as he expected'

un))n

A Delightful and Comfortable Holiday Home overlooking the Hondon Valley.

Available throughout the year, with five air-conditioned bedrooms, Sleeping nine.

For further details www.fuentelargo.com

Or send an email to jean@fuentelargo.com

Or WhatsApp (00 34) 678090197

 **The following item is a remarkable tale unusually written in that it is by ten members of the Writers Circle - each taking it in turns to enlarge the story line, by inscribing and adding about two hundred words before passing it on for the next author to develop the plot.**

At the end of it, those taking part are named.

MISSING

Chapter One

It had been a long week for teachers Gerry and Elaine Pritchard. That Friday's parents' evening had brought the usual array of characters, ranging from the deeply-concerned and pushy to the blasé and mild-mannered. However, conversation at school over the last few days had been dominated by the sudden disappearance of their colleague Susan Watkins.

"Sue is so lovely," Elaine sighed as she handed Gerry a large glass of wine. "It must be awful for her family."

"Yes, everyone likes her. Some of my students have commented about how good she is; we don't get much positive feedback on our teaching skills!"

"Let's just hope she turns up soon, it's very upsetting." She drained over half her glass in one go. Gerry followed suit, then patted the wine bottle. "Enjoy, Elaine, we've earned it!" He got up to draw the curtains, but as he approached the window, he noticed lights in the fields behind the back garden. Gerry peered into the darkness. "That's strange ..."

"Is someone out there?" Elaine asked anxiously, before joining her husband.

"It's probably nothing, love, but I thought I saw lights. It's a chilly night for camping! I'll get the torch and take a look ... "

As Gerry made his way across the fields his heart was hammering wildly, terrified of what he might, or might not find. As he approached the source of the lights his fears proved accurate.

"Susan!" he breathed, "what on earth are you doing here?"

"Oh Gerry!" replied Susan, sobbing. "I don't know what to do, I can't take this anymore!"

"For God's sake Susan" exclaimed Gerry, "you'll ruin everything if you're seen! I thought we'd agreed that you'd stay there in the Boat House until I could work out a way to get us out of this mess! We just need a little more time".

"I know Gerry, but it was so scary, it is so cold and dark down there, and I heard some sounds outside. I looked out of the small window and saw a shadow. I was terrified and kept thinking what would happen if they find me. I wanted to call you Gerry, but I can't. Then I got totally panicked and ran out, the only thing I could think of was that I had to talk to you. So I ran up here behind your house in the hope that you would see the light of my torch".

"Yes, but it was just luck that I saw it, you have to go back, you can't be out here, people are looking for you Susan".

"I'll never go back!" she was sobbing "It is so scary in there".

Susan looked up to him with tearful eyes and an overwhelming passion overtook him as he held her close and longingly. It was in this one fleeting moment that he realised he loved her.

Suddenly Gerry heard voices. He switched off his torch and raised his index finger to his lips in alarm. In the stillness of the cold night, the two people too frightened to even breath for fear of being heard, crouched in the shadow of the trees. Men's voices grew louder as their flashlights show the way through the orchard lighting the trees in an eerie hue. Soon the men were almost on top of them as Gerry and Sue heard the crackling of the crisp dry leaves under the men's feet. As they crouched like frightened rabbits in refuge their eyes met making that connection again.

The men turned in another direction and they were in the clear, Gerry told Sue to run back to the shelter and wait for him there. He desperately wanted to go with her but that was not in the plan yet, that he was beginning to formulate.

"Gerry, where the hell have you been?" Elaine sounded anxious. "The police have just been here, and I had to answer some questions about Susan. They want to talk to you, but I said you'd gone out in the back fields because we saw some lights, they've sent some officers to investigate."

At that point the local news headlines on the TV that had been blaring away in the background, caught both their attention ...

Chapter Two

Although the weather had been kind and it had been a pleasant Autumn evening, Joe McKenney, a lonely man who lived on his own, and frequently known as Jock, was cold and a little disappointed. This was the third night his poaching habit had been curtailed and once more he sat quietly and unseen on the side of the fast-flowing stream looking at the activity of the various people wandering on the hill. Especially as there were Police, he thought it was prudent not to be involved in his normal nightly activity.

He saw the small boathouse a little way along the river bank, belonging to the house a little further up the hill. It was normally empty but had been occupied by a single lady for the past few days. With perfect hearing developed by his nightly excursions, he had become aware of her name as Susan, by the discussions with a man who visited her on odd occasions. They had been together again tonight but up near the house and had heard the heated argument telling her to go back and wait for him.

He watched and waited until all was once again calm and the regular night sounds of rooting animals and the call of the odd nightjar assured him that there were no intruders nearby, but he'd lost interest in poaching; now there was something very strange going on and he wanted to find out just what it was all about. Besides, the fear in the young woman's voice had stirred emotions in him long since forgotten so that he found himself feeling rather protective toward her.

Guessing that she would have returned to the boathouse he made his way along the river bank ever watchful. And was relieved when he saw the Police who had been wandering around the grounds leave the property. He was carrying his traps and bag and it would be very difficult to explain those away if stopped by some overly zealous official at this time of night.

As he reached the boathouse, he could see a very dim glow illuminating a small window – so she was there then.   He tiptoed along the decking until he reached a small side door.   He paused gripping the handle, wondering what he was going to say to the girl.

A board creaked behind him a split second before he felt a blow to his head and as the girl's voice called out fearfully "Who's there?"

But Jock never got the chance to reply nor to find out why the woman called Susan was hiding in that boathouse in the first place. The well-aimed blow to his head had successfully knocked him out and with a moaning sound he was falling to the ground.

Although Gerry had returned to the house, he was worried and retrieving his baseball bat from the bedroom had managed to leave without Elaine asking further questions as she was intrigued by the programme on the television. When he saw Joe making his way to where Susan was, he managed to get there before him.

Dropping the bat which bounced on the floor and rolled to one side as he tried to catch the falling man, wondering who he was and why he had been creeping around the boathouse. Had the man known who was hiding in there and why? Were they found out?

He was too distracted by his thoughts and the man's heavy body slid through his hands, hitting the wooden floor with a loud thump. Inside the boathouse he heard Sue crying out fearfully. With a last confused look at the man he quickly stepped over the unconscious body and knocked on the door "Sue, it's me, let me in."

The door was yanked open and Sue flung herself into Gerry's arms. "I was scared out of my mind, I thought I heard someone lurking around outside. I am so glad you are here!" Gerry held her, allowing her to calm down, but he knew they did not have time for this. With the police inquiring at his house and the unconscious stranger here, who could wake up any time, they needed a new plan and fast.

They kissed and cuddled but he knew there was no time and sitting her down he told her he must get back otherwise people will be looking for him. Reluctantly he pushed the door open with his back … blowing her a kiss he let the door shut and turned to go back to the house.

Chapter Three

Manor Spring School was a public school opened some 200 years ago by a wily local entrepreneur called Dawlish. The school was aimed at attracting the sons of local minor gentry and successful farmers. It had succeeded and within a few years was showing Mr Dawlish a healthy profit.

The school continued to thrive and, in the seventies, opened its door to young ladies. It had an outstanding Ofsted rating which had been achieved under its current headmaster Mr or as he liked to be known Professor, Adam Dalgleish.
A title the governors were apt to overlook given the school's reputation.

Dalgleish was a strict man and would not stand for any liaisons between the members of staff. Two unmarried teachers had recently been dismissed for falling pregnant. No scandal was going to affect his school.

He had become aware of the affair between Gerry and Sue Watkins and had decided to deal with the matter personally and went in search to see what was happening at the old boat house. Treading on the baseball bat, then it rolled away from his foot, he stooped and picked it up.

Earlier Joe McKenney had been in the wrong place and had felt the kiss of the baseball bat. Gerry was half turned and ready to leave only to be the bats second victim that evening.

Dalgleish rolled both bodies over the jetty edge and into the fast-flowing stream. He watched them disappear into the darkness.

Sue Watkins screamed but was silenced by Dalgleish holding a finger to his lips. "Now Miss Watkins, what are we to do with you?"

Sue caught her breath. What was she going to do now?

After being let go from Manor Spring School, she had carefully hidden her pregnancy away from prying eyes and questions. Now here she was, confronted by the man who had not only cut her career short but had also thrown her lover's body into the river. Was he alive? She had no idea.

"What do you want from me, Adam"? she asked shocked and tearful.

"I want to know what's going on" he retorted.

"Gerry and I were going to go away so we could be together but now you've put paid to that! I hope you get locked up for what you've done, and the keys thrown away. How dare you end my career then murder the man I love".

Sue was angry and sobbing hard now, unable to control herself. Adam Dalgleish grabbed a rope that was hanging on the wall in the boat house. He tussled with Sue, wrapping her arms and hands behind her back and tying them tight with the rope. As he removed his belt, Sue gasped in horror at the thoughts running through her head. However, Adam man-handled her onto a dining room chair, strapping her to it with his belt.

As he stood in the open doorway, his large frame filling it, his bulky shadow was blocking the natural light from the dimly lit room.

"I'll be back" he said and promptly left, closing the door behind him.

Chapter Four

Hearing was the first sense to return. The thundering sound of the water snapped back the rest of his thoughts. Jock found himself rolling uncontrollably down the river. What the hell he thought.

He quickly kicked out his legs, pushing himself off the rocks as the water forced him along this dark watery hell. The searing pain in his head did little to vanquish Jock's spirit. He was a survivor. Jock lay on his back atop his poachers bag, sailing faster and faster downstream. The bloated dead rabbits inside the bag had acted as a float saving his life.

The full moon shone between the trees as Jock, pushed by the current, headed towards a fork in the river. He let himself go with the flow, spying a chance. A great old weeping willow ahead. Jock grabbed the branches with both hands and abruptly hung there, like a big wet bear who had just missed the trout. Jock caught his breath. He had one thing in mind. Revenge.

Elaine sat in the living room staring at the television, but her attention was not focused on the breaking news report. Her husband had promised to come back to the house. However, that was well over an hour ago and there was still no sign of Gerry. She wondered if the police would be back to ask any more questions to which she had no answers.

Turning away from the flickering pictures she picked up the empty bottle of wine, and only just managed to resist the urge to smash it against the wall. Elaine was toying with the idea of going out into the night to conduct her own investigations when there was a loud banging on the door. She rubbed her face, blinked a few tears away and found a familiar figure looking at her with an inscrutable expression.

"Oh, it's you," She managed a half smile. Dalgleish had left the boat house and now wanted words with Elaine thinking with Gerry out of the way it could be an interesting evening.

Professor Dalgleish smiled at her and said "Is Gerry home? I rather wanted a word with him".

"No", replied Elaine, I'm not sure where he is but he should be back soon. Would you like to wait here for him? You can join me in a glass of wine if you like?"

"Actually, Elaine, I suppose I should really tell you what this is all about, as it also concerns you", said Dalgleish, smiling benignly at her. However, something about the cold, smiling way he looked at her rang alarm bells in Elaine's head, and she felt a faint frisson of fear.

"Sit down, Professor," she said, "and I'll get another glass and a fresh bottle. We can wait for Gerry together. Make yourself comfortable, I won't be a minute."

She made her way to the kitchen and quickly looked to check that the key was still in the back door. Something was wrong, very wrong, and while she wasn't sure how to rationalise it she trusted her instinct and quietly opened the back door, intending to make her escape.

"Where are you going, Elaine?" said a quiet voice behind her. Dalgleish made a grab for her but she slipped through his grasp, and ran through the open kitchen door, screaming for help and slamming the door behind her.

There was nobody out there, she was wondering where she might run, knowing that he was just behind her. The only place that she can could think about was the boat house. Elaine was running for her life, she knew she could hide from the professor there and could feel the panic rising inside her.

Then she was almost at her destination and ran as fast as she could. Stumbled through the door and closed it behind her. She was terrified and wondering what would happen next, then she heard something behind her. Turned and found Susan tied to a chair.

Chapter Five.

It was gone midnight and Detective Inspector Charlene Goddard, Charlie as she was affectionately known to her friends, sat brooding over the evidence that had been collated by her team that evening. She picked up the next statement that was on her desk and the name Adam Dalgleish suddenly shot out of the handwritten statement and hit her hard in the stomach. Her mouth went dry and her heart started to pound as a cold sweat enveloped her body. The name made her cringe and brought up long lost horrendous memories.

Having been one of the first intakes of girl pupils at Manor Spring School herself some thirty years ago she remembered Adam Dalgleish as the lecherous Physical Education Teacher. She could see him now a large framed man who fancied himself as a bit of a rugby player, greasy slicked back hair and the repulsive smell of 'his' aftershave; always coming in the changing rooms and brushing up against young adolescent girls, staring menacingly at them with leering eyes.

She was a victim yet despite her distinguished career she never ever spoke a word of how she was abused. She felt ashamed and guilty, it was all her fault, that is what he said and at twelve years old she believed him. How he managed to work his way up to Head Teacher she would never know. The title Professor made her decidedly sick yet curious that he could have reached such high status. She despised him and she realised that now was the time to seek justice.

Charlie was disturbed from her horrific memories and that smell of his repugnant aftershave, by her Sergeant as he entered her office. "Ma'am, we've just had a report from Mrs Wilson, 'Manor Farm House' saying that there are people wandering around her garden and there are lights on in the boat house belonging to the people next door. She's eighty-three years old, on her own and sounding very worried!"

Charlie gathered her thoughts and resumed as much normality as possible getting her mind on the case of Susan Watkins, the missing school teacher. Deciding to go and look for herself.

She strapped herself in the driver's seat of the Police car as her Sergeant sat in the front beside her. She was an experienced driver with 20 years or more in the Force and had been on many blue light emergencies. In no time at all they were across the other side of town and soon in the quiet dark country lanes flanked by trees, stone walls and bushes.

Suddenly through the trees they caught site of a shadowy figure in the car headlights. They both saw it at the same time, and at first thought it was some sort of animal, but then when the headlights caught sight of it again, they realised it was the outline of a man stumbling from tree to tree as though drunk.

Charlie stopped the vehicle and they got out to investigate. They soon caught up with him. Although it was dark, and with only their torch lights to see, they soon realised he was injured, blood dripping from his head and his clothes soaking wet. He looked alarmed at the site of the two police officers and tried to scramble away but the pain was too much for him to bear and he collapsed in front of them.

Instantly Charlie recognised Gerry and wondered how he had got into such a state.

An ambulance was called, and Charlie told her Sergeant to go with him to the Hospital and let her know the instance he was conscious again. She was no doctor but in the back of her mind she did not know if he would live or die, the injury to his head looked severe.

Chapter Six

Charlie, made her way to the Boat House alone; as she entered the last corner in the road she turned all the lights off in the car and drove slowly along the track. She stopped the vehicle at the back of some trees and went by foot the rest of the way. A dim light was still lighting the interior and she tried to peer through the window, but it was dirty, cracked and growing in mould.

The moon was bouncing off the water from the river and it was then that she noticed blood on the wooden veranda and along the railings. 'What has been going on here?' she thought to herself.

She then saw the baseball bat, she took out her mobile phone and took several photos of where it lay then she put on her latex glove and examined the bat. It was spattered in blood and her heart thumped wildly at the repugnant smell of aftershave, violet and mint sweetened with mace hit her hard. "It's him he's been here I shall never forget that smell". She took three deep breaths and gained control of her feelings and put down the bat.

She then closed her hand around the handle of the wooden door turning it slowly as she gently pushed the door with her arm; the door creaked open and stood before her was Elaine. Charlie's trained eyes immediately scouted the room and in the dimly lit hue of the boathouse she saw Susan by a chair now released from her bonds.

The three women stood there in momentary silence and in that split second it was as if they could read each other's minds - to seek revenge on 'Professor' Adam Dalgleish.

**

Adam Dalgleish thought it was pointless chasing after her it would only raise suspicion two people chasing. He turned to the bottle of wine and thought of the joy the rest of the evening could bring and sat down and waited.

He made himself comfortable and with total joy enjoyed the mellow taste of the red liquid. Finally he thought it was time to go after his prey, and left by the kitchen door feeling the excitement building inside of him as he planned on the evening's entertainment. It was a movement near the river which stopped him, turning his head in that direction.

Dalgliesh stood motionless. He was looking over the ground and down towards the flowing water. He was trying to understand what the movement was that he had seen out of the corner of his eyes when most of his thoughts were on Elaine. His eyes slowly adjusted to the shadowy light from the moon and he thought it was just the movement of the trees blowing in the gentle wind.

His eyes widened, he suddenly felt a little sick as with a jolt to his heart he saw the blue and knew instantly it was the reflection from the dome of a police light, which was extinguished on the roof of a car. Why were they here and with no lights on … the thought flashed through his mind?

Chapter Seven

The Professor was not the only person to see the car, although for Jock it was a blessing. He had lain still for some time, now out of the water recovering from his ordeal, when the car had come to a stop close by. He peered through the covering of the reeds to see it standing a little way from him up the steep bank. He thoughtfully watched as the one lady policewoman stepped out of the car and walked up the path towards the boat house.

Dragging himself out of the water and feeling the moisture soaking his clothing giving him the feeling of being very cold. First though, he must get rid of the kit that on most nights gave him a living, but he did not think the police would accept that as an excuse. With sadness he pushed the familiar bag deeper into the reeds knowing it would be unlikely if he would be able to find it again

**

Gerry lay in his hospital bed with a maelstrom of thoughts flying around in his heavily bandaged head. It was so hard to think with the constant throbbing behind his eyes. He'd gleaned from overheard conversations that he'd been admitted suffering from hypothermia and suspected concussion from a head wound but try as he may he could not recall anything after finding some snooper at the boathouse. He broke out into a sweat when he remembered that, fearful of this unknown intruder and still carrying the baseball bat he'd taken from the house, he'd lashed out without thinking and knocked him down.

How did he end up with a head wound? Had someone hit him too? A niggling thought settled uneasily in his mind. Could Elaine have followed him and found him with Susan? She had a hot temper but surely not; he just couldn't believe that she would attack him, but if not her who, and how was he going to explain away his present situation? His little game was up and he knew it. He stood to lose his wife, his home and his job not to mention his reputation, and on top of everything else he could be prosecuted for assault or worse. He groaned, "Oh, what a bloody mess."

He heard the door to his room open and his heart skipped a beat as a uniformed policeman entered accompanied by a petite woman in plain clothes. She smiled disarmingly "Good day to you Sir, I'm Detective Inspector Goddard and we just have a few questions for you if you are feeling up to it."

**

Susan felt awkward being alone with Elaine in the boathouse and started chatting nervously. 'So, what do you think about Charlie's plan for revenge, Elaine? Do you think it will work?'

Charlie had to leave them after having received a phone call from her Sergeant. She had told them there was a suspect who was in the hospital and had recovered and needed to be interviewed.

So, Charlie had quickly explained her plan to unmask Dalgleish for who he really was and then she rushed out, oblivious to the fact she was leaving a pregnant mistress alone with the wife of her lover. Susan wondered now if Elaine suspected anything but couldn't read her expression. She thought how lucky she was that her pregnancy wasn't showing yet.

"Well, to be honest I am not sure, why we need a revenge plan. He didn't do anything to me. I am starting to think I overreacted, when I ran away like a crazy person." Elaine looked at Susan with a blank face. "Anyway, what do you want revenge for, Susan? Why did he leave you tied up in this boathouse and what were you doing here in the first place?"

Susan didn't want to be in Elaine's company any longer or answer her questions. She was carrying the illegitimate child of Elaine's husband and trying to hide her pregnancy from this woman. Susan made an excuse that she had to get home and promptly left the boat house.

She had no car as Gerry had brought her, so she started walking. She was still in a state of shock that Adam Dalgleish had not only tied her up but hit and possibly killed two men with a baseball bat. Her mind went over the event that had occurred that night.

As she was walking, Jock stumbled out of the undergrowth and fell into her path. Susan let out a startled gasp as she looked at this bedraggled man. He was soaked to the skin; his clothes were torn, and his face was covered with blood from a head wound.

"Please help me" said Jock. Susan was a little nervous and not sure what to do. She didn't know who he was, had no transport and her phone was dead.

"Who are you and what happened?" Susan asked him.

"I'm Joe McKenney from Sunny Side, about a mile from here and I was hit over the head by someone at the boat house. I don't feel too good at the minute".

"Oh, thank God" said Susan, "I thought you were dead after falling into the river".

She remembered that old Mrs Wilson lived at Manor Farm House, a little further down the lane.

"Let's get you to Mrs Wilson's just over there and we can call an ambulance".

It was while they waited for the ambulance that Susan finally took stock of her position and realised it could not continue. Tomorrow she would rid herself of the situation and return to her home town in Scotland, where there were family and she would be able to put the recent events behind her and look after the child she was expecting and would be a constant reminder of her time in this place.

Chapter Eight

D.I Charlene Goddard turned off the audio recording and ended the interview. Gerry was sitting bolt upright in his hospital bed looking pale and drawn. She felt she had pushed him far enough tonight and thanked him for his statement. He had been talking for more than an hour. She had what she needed.

What a mess! As she already had surmised after the talk with Elaine Pritchard, also Susan and now Gerry, the prime suspect for the attempted murders and holding Susan captive was indeed the same man who had assaulted her all those years ago.

Shoving her recorder and signed statement in her bag she marched back to the car. 'Karma' had finally caught up with Adam Dalgleish. Charlie phoned her station. There was no time to waste. She needed an arrest warrant. That bastard was finally going to pay.

Elaine was her husband's final visitor in hospital that day. They sat holding hands in silence for what seemed like a long time. When their eyes met, she knew that they needed to focus on putting the trauma behind them, and not to worry about trying to tie up all the loose ends. Some should be left to unravel. At that moment there seemed to be an unspoken agreement that it was worth trying to rebuild their relationship...

Two months later the Pritchard couple found themselves once again chatting over a bottle of wine at the end of an arduous week at school. They had avoided discussing Dalgleish's court case and Susan's departure to start a new life in Scotland. As the pair had started putting the broken pieces of their lives back together, a new picture was slowly forming. When Elaine noticed lights in the field beyond the garden that Friday evening, she said nothing. The woman bit her lip and drew the curtains tightly, before pouring them both another stiff drink.

Authors (in alphabetical order):

Brian Baggerley - Percy W. Chattey-
Sarah Dawkins RN - Debbie Freeman-
Caroline Goss - Tarika Gradva –
Karen Kopczynska -Trudy Le Beau –
Richard Seal - S. J. Tarsus.
"""""

Three diverse stories by different writers based on the word 'fear'.

Fear

Trudie Le Beau

Thankful to be home after a busy day at work she turned her key in the lock but stopped, rooted to the spot by the familiar smell of after shave that greeted her through the half open door. Heart hammering, she quietly pulled the door too and removed her key struggling to breath and fighting down the panic that was threatening to overwhelm her. She willed her legs to carry her down the path and onto the street where she stumbled away from the house as fast as her trembling limbs would allow, all the while waiting for the familiar hand to clamp onto her shoulder or her throat and drag her back into that nightmare world that she had tried so hard to forget.

She was relieved to reach the comfort of the well-lit high street and now dared to stop in order to get her breath back before making her way to the nearest coffee shop. She selected a seat that was tucked away in a corner behind an artificial palm and ordered a black coffee thinking that maybe what she really needed was a stiff drink.

Still trembling she clutched the hot drink to her chest "What to do – what to do?"   Absolutely at a loss she decided to ring the only real friend she had.   The ring tone seemed to go on forever before Laura at last picked up "Hi Mo. Everything alright?"

"He's here!" It was hard for Maureen to get the words out as they meant his presence was a reality, but she persevered, "He's here. He's in my house, I smelt his aftershave.   I'm in Romano's and I don't know what to do and..."

It was obvious to Laura that her friend was really distraught "Just stay where you are Mo, I'll be there in fifteen minutes. Just stay there and don't do anything ... ok."

Mo nodded as the phone went dead.

Laura's head was swimming as she cast her mind back to the first time she had met Mo when she came to work at the depot and they had formed a friendship almost immediately, mostly because Laura had felt sorry for the newcomer.   She had been such a timid thing, almost afraid of her own shadow. Gradually as their friendship had deepened Maureen had opened up to her, and the reasons for her reticence to engage with others soon became apparent.

She had lived in a children's home from the age of ten as both her parents had been killed in an accident and there were no other family members willing to take her in. She'd had to leave the home at the age of sixteen and fend for herself and it was while she was alone that she'd met Gary. He was eleven years older than her and he'd taken the place of the family she hadn't had. In the beginning he was kind and caring and she had been really happy for the first time in years, but gradually as she matured and wanted to be a little more independent from him he had become more and more controlling and was consumed with jealousy of any contact she'd had with male colleagues, so much so that in the end he'd prevented her from going to work. She had become a virtual prisoner and any attempt to thwart him in any way resulted in any dispute being settled with his fists and threats against her life.

That had all ended five years ago when he was arrested for attacking a policeman summoned by a worried neighbour during one of these disputes. Taking advantage of his absence Maureen had plucked up enough courage to run, and once free she had never looked back, covering her tracks as best she could, but now it seemed he had caught up with her, but how? How, after five years could he possibly have tracked her down? Maybe Mo was mistaken, maybe something had spooked her.

In Romano's Laura found Mo hidden in the corner still clutching her now cold coffee, looking up at her with naked fear in her eyes. She was overcome with compassion for her friend and raged inside that any one human being could instil such terror in another. "You're coming home with me Mo and tomorrow we'll do whatever is needed to sort this out once and for all."

Unresisting, Maureen linked arms with her friend as she was lead out into the night hoping against hope that Laura's confident words of reassurance meant that she could finally be free.

""""

Entering 'Hondon de los Frailes' from the Albatera Road

Development of Fear

Percy Chattey

At thirty years of age Federica Ebonique Antonetta
Rasmas was a doctor in the field of nuclear energy
working in a large airy laboratory in control of a very
important experiment. Her parents came from a small
village in Eastern Europe and as a child she would
roam over the footpaths of the mountains in which
her house nestled, like so many others nearby.
She was named after her grandmother which is a
little puzzling as her elder was a white European.
However, Ebonique's second name means black which
originates from an uncle on her father's side. The
story in the family was that one hundred or so years
previously, one of her forbearers had taken a gypsy
woman who was from an African Continent tribe
touring through the area at the time, resulting in a
baby boy.

The boy was left to die on the side of the track when
the African group moved on. It was Ebonique's Great
Grandfather who late one morning, when he was
returning after collecting firewood from the forest
which covered the landscape. He came to a stop as he
heard a noise to the side of the road. A little earlier

he had noticed his two dogs who were racing in front, were interested in a pile of rags laying in the scrub grass near some bushes. He was stooping down when he found inside the bundle of old clothing a very hungry baby boy.

The child was taken in by the family, where they brought it up as one of their own. He became one of them taking on the family name of Rasmas.

Ebonique was a progressive young woman in her nature, her direct ancestry was more evident than other members of the family. Her approach about everything she did was more outgoing than her kinfolk and she strived to do things differently, especially in her work.

She had been interested for some time in propulsion. The means of developing a small nuclear-powered unit as a way of propelling all manner of vehicles, from the large and especially the small. She had visions of a new type of small personal carrier silently scuttling around the streets and felt certain the prize was within her grasp.

The thought had first come to her consideration when she was studying through her college years and she developed an interest in how submarines, vessels and other large plants used fission to produce a result.

After years of studying the subject Ebonique became well known for her knowledge and was recognised as the top expert in her field. There was excitement spreading amongst the specialists as it became known that she was on the edge of a breakthrough. People would gather in groups, in bars and elsewhere discussing the possibility of a car which did not need fuel once it was built.

However, her work was very secretive and although the media tried to find out what her real progress was, they were none the wiser but they still reported on rumours and the small snippets of information they could glean.

The powerful people funding the development were anxious to move the project on. Ebonique on the other hand knew there were items and small problems which needed to be resolved before she was ready to display her work, which was to be in a secure laboratory.

The pressure from her sponsors to exhibit what she had achieved was too great, and after a heated discussion she agreed to hold a demonstration of her findings.

Crowds gathered in the small building where chairs had been laid out for the visitors to be able to follow the result of her work. Scientists, news people and the individuals funding the project, some were standing in groups others were seated with microphones, smart phones with tablets on display.

The small machine she had produced was displayed on a bench behind a thick glass screen. On the clear partition embedded in the glass was the letters of her initials 'FEAR' this name was repeated on a sign above her new development.

Ebonique was more interested in her work than public speaking. She appeared from the side and there was excited clapping and cheering. Looking through the glass at the audience, murmuring a few words of greeting as she smiled. Promptly standing to one side and holding out both her hands in gesture to show what she had developed.

Everyone went quiet as she went to a control board with flashing different coloured lights and a large white button to the centre. Her hand hovered over it. She turned, once again smiling at the audience as she pressed it.

At first nothing happened. Then a large red display sign above the project with her initials 'FEAR' on it started to flash. There was a rumbling noise and the machine started to shake. A siren sounded its piercing sound drowning out all other noises.

People were now looking at each other, the clamour of the warning was shattering and deafening. Terror spread amongst the visitors as they quickly stood up knocking chairs over in their haste. They were being encouraged to quickly leave the building by the security staff.

Bang!!! The explosion destroyed the building.

᭐᭐᭐᭐᭐

Fear – The Walk Home

Caroline Goss

How she wished she'd passed her driving test the first time as she walked to the pub wrapped up in her padded coat buttoned up to the top and scarf shrouding her face from the cold northerly wind that was biting at her core. The street lights in the village were haloed in a warm orange glow along the lane to one side and on the other side were the beech woods that they used to play in as children. Branching off the lane was the new housing estate. She remembers when they built it there was such an uproar from the villagers as the trees in the old wood were pulled down and chopped up one by one replaced by tarmac roads flanked by modern houses of brick and mortar.

Finally, she reached the 'Hare and Hounds'. Her usual gathering of friends were there and it didn't take them long before they were all on their second round of drinks, as they sat on the pew like wooden seats with their thinning cushions worn through over the years by the patrons.

"Come on Sasha, you must know a ghost story especially working in the funeral parlour?" jested Mike as his beer nearly flew out over the rim of his glass as he pointed it towards her.

Sasha didn't believe in ghosts probably because she worked with those that had passed away, but she got caught up in the moment and remembered a ghost story that had been on the television a while ago. She began to recall it as her friends listened attentively to every word as they were supping their drinks.

Sasha carried on............ 'So, his mother told him not to go into the attic, but her son had said, 'no I won't go anymore because the old lady in the attic with the knitting has told me she has to go now!" .... Sasha carried on her story making a lot of it up because she couldn't quite remember how it finished. Her friends were making spooky noises at the end of her story as they all laughed hysterically.

Another round of drinks and then Mike got serious, "I have a ghost story to tell." Sasha took note of how his tone changed she was very sensitive and noticed things like that especially since taking a counselling course to help with grieving families in the Funeral Parlour.

Mike continued, " Well, as you know, I live with my parents in one of the new houses on the estate. Our house was one of the first ones to be built a couple of years ago. I was nearly 16 when we moved. I have my own room and after a couple of months I kept waking up at night and hearing horses. You know how they bray and whinny; well at first I didn't really take any notice but when it continued I asked Mum if there were any stables nearby, she said no. One particular night I had a really weird dream about a Roman legionnaire on his chariot led by two powerful black stallions. The horses suddenly stopped from their canter throwing out the soldier onto the stony road. The Celts were soon there wielding their long swords as the soldier tried to defend himself, they cut off his arm and left him for dead. In the meantime, the thunderous roar of the iron wheels of the chariot drawn by the horses on the slabbed Roman road was getting louder and louder. I suddenly felt like it was there in the room with me it was getting closer and I woke up with a start.

The next day I decided to do a bit of research and found out that the Roman legions fought here in the Battle of Medway in AD 43 on the lands of a Celtic tribe which is exactly where these woodlands are. Legend has it that there is a ghostly figure of a Roman Soldier riding his chariot through the woods as he searches aimlessly for his battalion. There have been many sightings of the one armed legionnaire on his chariot, so you'd better watch out when you go home tonight past those woods Sasha!"

Mike captivated his slightly inebriated audience with his ghoulish tale as they listened in. 'Ooooh spooky,' said Simon making light of it all and the others all joined in with ruckus laughing and eerie ghostly sounds.

At the end of the evening the friends all said goodnight and went their separate ways except Mike and Sasha as they both lived in the same direction. With muffled speech through her scarf Sasha asked Mike if the story he told was true. "Ha Ha no," he replied mockingly, "You're so gullible you'd believe anything." She looked up at him in a quizzical manner. He didn't say anything, but he spoke volumes with his eyes and she knew it was true or had she had too much to drink?

The couple walked out of the village and towards the estate where Mike said goodbye, but before he did, he raised his voice and shouted out quite unexpectedly "Boo!" Sasha let out a distorted scream from under her scarf as her eyes widened in alarm. "Ha Ha that made you jump; see you next week that is if the one-armed Roman Soldier hasn't got you first!" She raised her eyebrows as she half laughed "Yes, see you next week Mike."

Her dark shadow moulded the cracked pavement under the last street light on the road as she began the rest of her journey home. The tale of the soldier played on her mind and her vivid imagination was taking her into a surreal world of non-rational visions as shapes and forms in the hanging branches of the beech wood across the road were watching her every move.

She tried to get back into her safe zone telling herself it was just foolish thoughts and there were no such things as ghosts! However, the more she tried the harder it was becoming as she could now make out the dark shapes amongst the trees of Roman soldiers and the rustling of footsteps amongst the leaves. A cold chill tingled her spine and she quickened her pace.

She approached the small hamlet of houses where she lived and had to make a hurried decision whether or not to take the back way through the road of garages to the back gate or continue along the lane adjacent to the woods and their haunting apparitions amongst the shady branches and tree trunks.

She went left which took her down the back of the garages along a badly concreted lane. She began to feel a little less anxious as she saw the familiar cars parked outside her neighbours' garage and the tall wooden gate at the back of her parent's home. Then suddenly without warning the wind picked up and she heard it, she heard the rhythmic sound of horses as their hooves hit the ground and the distinctive sound of the chariot as the hard metal wheels thundered towards her.

Fear overwhelmed her and she ran, her heart was pounding, adrenaline coursing through her veins. She could think of nothing except the noise behind her, getting louder as it was getting closer.

Not even daring to look behind her for fear of what she might see she reached the gate, unlatched it with shaking hands and slammed it behind her. She stood there for a while catching her breath and suddenly realised she could still hear the noise of the chariot and horses resounding in her ears. Her heart beat faster again but feeling safe now in her fortress she peered through a broken knot in the wooden fence; there was nothing there but an empty Coke can caught up in the wind rolling recklessly down the back road in amongst a shower of autumnal leaves. Relief swamped her entire body as she realised how ridiculous she was acting and gave out a quiet sigh. Sasha walked down the back path to the kitchen door and as she opened the back door, she looked back up the path and in a split second saw someone or something standing at the back gate.

Another tale from Richard who was a founder member of the Writers Circle in 2017

Catacombs

Richard Seal

The Paris cafe was very busy on a chilly Saturday afternoon in November, the two students knew that they were lucky to have the chance to grab a corner table just as another couple was leaving. Belinda did a double-take on taking a sip of her expresso. She always managed to forget how strong coffee was in France until the next time that she had one. Her friend Liz seemed to be neglecting her tea in favour of poring over the huge map of Paris.

"This font is so small, Bel, I think I'm going to need some reading glasses soon. Or possibly even a white stick!"

"Let's have a look." Belinda took the map, and struggled to get to grips with it. "It might be easier if someone made the city a bit smaller, don't you think?"

"The entrance to the catacombs is supposed to be somewhere around here, but it looks like it might be tricky to find."

"Let's keep trying, I would really like to visit them." Belinda enthused.

"Me too, they sound macabre, but fascinating."

At this point, a young man approached their table. His French accent was strong, but his English was very good "Excuse me, ladies, my name is Pierre. I was nearby and could not help overhearing your conversation. I think I can be of some assistance."

Belinda spoke first. "Thanks, Pierre. I am Belinda and this is my friend Liz. Can you tell us how to find the catacombs?"

"Better still, would you allow me to escort you to them? When you have both finished your drinks of course."

The man led the two women off the beaten track and down various small side streets, where there suddenly seemed to be a dearth of tourists. Liz caught Belinda's eye, and they exchanged frowns briefly, before Pierre suddenly came to a halt close to an alley, behind a row of parked cars. "Here we are. This will do nicely."

Liz glanced down at the map again. "I thought that the official entrance is at Avenue du Colonel Henri Rol-Tanguy. This isn't the place, surely? Where have you taken us?"

"You don't want to waste time going there - the queues are enormous, there are tourists everywhere; it's very expensive and they don't permit you to see very much. However, this is an unofficial entrance - there is much more freedom and fun this way." He lifted what appeared to be a manhole cover.

"Do you think we're mad?" asked Belinda. "You're asking us to disappear into this hole in the ground on your say so. We don't even know you. Besides, the catacombs are a dangerous place, aren't they, and isn't it illegal to enter like this too?"

"I understand your concerns of course, but there's no danger if you enter the tunnels with someone who is experienced, knows what they are doing and where they are going. I will, of course, be your guide."

"I don't know about this," Belinda turned to Liz, "What do you think?"

"Maybe. How much do you charge?"

"Look, let's say we talk about that at the end, when we're finished, and you can pay me what you think the tour was worth. Does that sound fair?"

"I guess so," said Belinda. "It might be a laugh."

The man checked that they both had torches, some water, and he handed Liz a map. "Keep hold of this, just in case. It is a bit cold down there - the temperature is always about fifteen degrees - so zip up your jackets."

As the women tentatively dropped down into the darkness, Liz landed awkwardly and felt a sharp, shooting pain in her ankle. She cried out, and stumbled heavily into the wall.

"Are you okay, Liz, watch your footing." Pierre extended a supporting hand.

"Now he tells me," she muttered to herself. "Yes, I'm fine - I think." She winced slightly when she put her foot down.

Belinda brushed herself down and shook her head. "That was quite a plunge, wasn't it?"

"Yes, it's a bit more rough and ready this way than the official route, I'm afraid."

"No kidding!" Liz rubbed her ankle gingerly.

"Switch on your flashlights, ladies, and have a good look around you. This is a place quite unlike any other, but there is nothing to fear - remember that the dead cannot do you any harm, unless you believe in ghosts ..." He grinned at them.

"Very funny!" Belinda felt an involuntary shiver run down her spine.

"The transfer of human remains from cemeteries to the tunnels began towards the end of the eighteenth century for public health reasons. The bones of approximately six million people are down here."

Belinda turned to her friend. "Perhaps we should have paid another visit to the Louvre instead of this place. It might have felt warmer too."

Liz spoke to Pierre. "It's okay, she's just kidding, but it is a bit creepy here don't you think?"

"This is better than spending your time looking at boring artworks alongside crowds of tourists, in my opinion. There is a special atmosphere, a unique vibe. Come, let me show you around."

Pierre started walking and beckoned them to follow. "Stay close to me and be very careful, some of the passageways are narrow and uneven, there is water in some places too."

The friends stayed quiet, focusing on where they were walking and trying not to let fear rise within. They lost track of the different forks that they were led down before the three of them froze on hearing muffled noises coming from somewhere behind them. "What was that?" Liz spoke breathlessly, "It scared the life out of me!"

Pierre stood still for a few moments, peered over his shoulder, and looked slightly anxious before replying. "Don't worry, I will go back and investigate. Stay where you are, please, and don't be afraid. I will be back shortly," The man had turned tail and disappeared into the darkness before the girls had time to object.

"Well, I don't know about you, Liz, but the day is not quite panning out the way I had expected it to."

"No .. I wish I had worn a warmer jumper too."

They stood for a while, moving their limbs to try to keep out the cold. Belinda noticed that her torch beam was getting weaker, and asked Liz to turn hers off to preserve the battery. She suggested they sit down. "I know it's not very comfortable, Liz, but my flat feet are starting to play up."

"When do you think Pierre is coming back, it feels like he's been gone for a long time."

"I'm sure we'll see him again soon," Belinda said dubiously, "I would check my watch if I had one."

"I haven't got one either. I'll have a look at my phone." She shook her head. "I have no signal down here."

"No surprise, I suppose. Mine is dead, I forgot to charge the battery this morning."

Liz put her hand on her friend's arm. "I don't have a good feeling about this. Are we going to be okay?"

"Of course, don't worry, you'll be safe with me. I'll fight off the undead if they decide to have a go at us .. " Belinda felt her voice cracking slightly. " Do you think we should try to find our own way back? Pierre gave you a map, didn't he?"

"Yes, but do you think we would be able to do it on our own? We could get lost."

Belinda directed her torch onto the map, but the diagrams were indistinct and confusing. "A bit of a challenge."

"Oh, this is hopeless, it's like reading hieroglyphics!" Liz was concerned that her voice was starting to sound shrill.

"Try to relax, let me study it for a while. I managed to survive several years of navigating across Europe sitting next to my impatient dad when I was younger."

"Reading a road map of Madrid or Rome is a bit more straightforward than a hand-drawn scrawl of underground passages!"

"Point taken." Belinda pored over the piece of paper, turning it round several times, and wracking her brain while her friend said nothing, occasionally sighing deeply.

Eventually the tension got to Liz. "We've got to do something to help ourselves, Bel, can you make any sense of that thing?"

"Well, I think I can work out our route, but we need to take it very slowly and I don't want the blame if things don't work out."

"Let's just go, I'll go mad if we wait here for our shady guide who might never return." As soon as she started walking, she was given a painful reminder of her injured ankle.

As Belinda led the way, Liz felt like they had been walking for hours and all the tunnels looked similar in the gloomy light. "Are you quite sure we are going the right way, none of the passageways were ankle-deep in water earlier?"

"Will you stop moaning, I don't like this any more than you do. Of course, I'm not sure where we are, but I'm doing my best. Feel free to take the map and lead the way if you think you can do a better job!"

"I'm sorry, Bel, I really I am. Take no notice of me. My ankle is so painful, and it's getting worse." She felt close to tears.

"It's okay, I understand. Come on, let's find a dry spot to rest. We've been trudging along for long enough." The friends huddled together in the cold. "I wonder if this is what a meditation retreat feels like - no home comforts and communion with the soul."

"This is no joke, Bel, I feel like we're in a horror film. Who knows when anyone will find us? Or if ... "

"Don't be silly, people come down here all the time I'm sure." Belinda tried to reassure her friend.

"In the official section, yes. But we're way off limits, somewhere in the miles of tunnels which stretch across the city. Nobody knows where we are."

"Pierre does, and he will be back eventually."

"Perhaps. He may be lost himself, of course, and even if he isn't, you're forgetting something very important." Liz's voice was grave. "We're no longer in the place where he left us ..."

They found a flat area and decided to try and get some sleep. Belinda's torch battery had gone flat, so they lay in the pitch darkness to preserve the power in Liz's flashlight.

"Have you got much water on you, Bel?"

"Just under half a bottle. And you?"

"Less than that. We need to ration what we've got left."

"And not think too much about food. I could murder some fish and chips!"

When Belinda opened her eyes, she felt very disorientated, not sure for a moment if she was dreaming. There was no telling what time it was or how long they had been down there. When she heard her friend stirring she touched her arm. It felt cold.

"How are you doing, Liz, bearing up?"

"Trying to. I feel very dry, so will have a sip of water in a minute. My ankle's throbbing."

"I've got a cracking headache myself. We're a perfect pair, aren't we? I don't think we'd better plan a trek in the Himalayas!"

"Bel, I don't want to die."

"We're temporarily misplaced in the Paris catacombs, not lost in outer space. You'll be sitting in your favourite chair on your hundredth birthday, impatiently waiting for your telegram. Just wait and see."

"Have you enjoyed your life?"

"What are you talking about? I'm only twenty years old, Liz, it's barely started!"

"If we don't make it out, which is possible, I would be interested to know how you would like to be remembered?"

Belinda sat in silence for a moment, for once short of a light-hearted response. "As someone who loved her family and friends, cared about people, made them laugh sometimes ... It's not every day that you get a chance to write your own epitaph is it? And what about you?"

"I don't know. Will they remember me? Do any of us really remember other people when they're gone, come to that?"

"Of course. We all live on in other people's hearts and minds. People like Shakespeare and de Vinci survive through their work, don't they?"

"I hear what you're saying, but I'm not so sure. I feel like I've done nothing yet, and I may not get the opportunity now. Life is so brief, barely a wave on the ocean." She sounded tearful.

"True, but let's enjoy the swim of life while we can - venture into the sea even when the red flag is flying!"

"Do you believe in the afterlife, Bel?"

"None of it makes much sense to me to be honest, it's a great story though."

"I am going to try praying when we stop next time, it might make me feel a bit better, more at peace with the situation."

The girls decided to have another attempt at finding their way to safety, but Liz needed her friend's assistance now as her ankle felt swollen. Both of them had finished their water and Liz's flashlight was getting weaker. Without discussing it, both were getting increasingly concerned and starting to feel weaker. Just as they were on the point of slumping to the ground, a familiar face appeared in front of them.

"Ladies! What a relief to find you at last."

"Pierre! What happened to you?" Both women were hugely relieved.

"The noises we heard were made by some other Cataphiles who had got lost, they needed my help. However, when I returned you had gone. It's really not a good idea to wander around and explore without a guide. Even with a map."

"You're not wrong! It felt like we had been waiting for you for ages though." Liz exclaimed.

"Time is so deceptive in this environment, you can lose perspective on it and start to feel confused."

"How long have we been in these tunnels, maybe twenty-four hours?"

"Around six I would say, not long enough to be concerned about hypothermia but too long for newcomers like yourselves. Let me get us out of here."

"What's a 'Cataphile' anyway?" Belinda asked as they walked.

"We are dedicated urban explorers who illegally tour the mines of Paris. There are quite a few of us, we love the life."

"It takes all sorts, I suppose. I prefer to play a game of Scrabble and have a hot drink myself."

It was not long before the three of them were clambering back up through the manhole and into the street. It was dark now. Pierre grinned. "We're lucky the police haven't found this entrance yet. It probably won't be long before they do, and it will be sealed off."

Belinda was aghast. "Sealed! Would we have been trapped down there?"

"Just temporarily. I would have found another way out eventually, but it might have taken a little while."

"Pierre, we were beginning to think that we might die," Liz added, "I was terrified by the time you arrived."

"Die? You'd be hard pressed to manage that with all the explorers around, not to mention police patrols. There's a spot fine if they catch you. In my opinion, you could last for several days down there before being at any risk of perishing. Starting to panic is the biggest danger or suffering from claustrophobia."

"I'm not sure whether to feel relieved by that statement or not!" said Belinda, "but one thing is for sure - it's been an experience that we're not likely to forget in a hurry."

Pierre was grateful to receive thirty Euros from the girls, despite their harrowing ordeal. "I hope this hasn't put you off exploring the tunnels, however you might want to visit the official catacombs next time - it's impossible to get lost in that area and you can see stacks of bones and so on. Enjoy the rest of your holiday." The man slinked away into the night.

"Bel, I'm not too keen on there being a next time. I think I'd prefer to visit the Arc de Triumph tomorrow, or perhaps the Sacre Coeur, if it's all the same with you. And then relax in a nice French restaurant."

"Good thinking, my friend. We should let the dead rest in peace. Let's go and find the nearest warm bar now and have a few drinks to dull your ankle pain!"

""""

Easter

Sarah Dawkins

There was a Cadbury's creme egg
Wrapper of yellow, blue and red
Hidden in the garden shed
Next to Johnny Walker, Red
All the children they did look
Under the table and a new book
T'was nearly dark when it was found
Wrapper, upon the ground
Grandad, there did sit
Laughing, picked and eating it!

Karen joined us this year with a smile on her face and itching fingers on a keyboard. In the past she has written articles for a Northern Ireland paper and while she loves the old country she is happily settled in Spain.

PANTS.

Karen Kopczynska

Mr Johnston looked out of his sitting room window at number 1A, Cherry Gardens, at the darkening sky, and wondered if it was safe to hang out the small basket of washing.

"Looks a bit like rain", he thought, then decided to take a chance anyway. He needed his best shirt and trousers dried, pressed and hung up, ready for the week ahead. If he didn't do it now, they wouldn't be ready in time, and then the whole week would be thrown into confusion.

Mr Johnston liked his week to be well planned, ordered and straightforward, as, in fact, he liked his life. A slight, thin man, he was a bookkeeper in a local company, where his days were tediously similar but reassuringly safe.

There was once a time when he had harboured secret little dreams of becoming something wild and free, like a poet, or an artist, but those days were long gone, trampled into the dust by the fear of failure.

On the rare occasions he allowed himself to admit it, his mother had been the one who had held up the flag of failure in front of him, frightening him with the thoughts of not having a decent place to live, or savings in the bank, or that one, a dry little holiday every year to the caravan park at Downing Strand.

Mr Johnston Senior had left his family shortly after his baby son was born, and it was rumoured he had run away with a burlesque dancer from a travelling show. Mr Johnston's mother had never come to terms with the fact that life can change on an impulse. It had never occurred to either Mr Johnston or his mother that whims can often be exciting, adventurous and fulfilling. His mother had died without ever having had any excitement of her own, all of which had taught Mr Johnston that in his world, whims were definitely to be avoided, and best left well alone.

Until now.

As he made his way to the courtyard where the communal washing line was located, he was aware of some activity in number 1C, the flat opposite his own. The flat had been empty for some time but had recently been occupied by a new tenant, a woman with wild, dark curling hair, and an inviting smile.

He sneaked a little glance towards the open window; he could hear music with a strong rhythm, and he caught sight of the woman swaying and dancing in time to the beat of the guitars and drums. She appeared to be lost in the moment, and something about her caught Mr

Johnston's imagination as quickly as an avalanche roaring down a mountain.

Shocked at his own reaction, he quickly pegged out his washing with trembling hands and went back indoors. From his kitchen, he was able to continue to watch the woman dance until the music ended.

Thoughts of her strong and sensual body flooded his mind.

Later he watched as she made her way to the courtyard, to hang up her own washing. It looked like a mass of wildly coloured fabrics, blues, reds and yellows, along with other little fripperies that women had – most of which he knew nothing about and tried not to think of.

Then he saw it. Scarlet satin with black lace edging. Looking like something that had no right to be there, in full view of everyone.

He waited for an hour and then decided that he had to make his move. He went to collect his washing, not caring that his clothes weren't quite dry. He bundled them into his basket, while managing to shockingly and silently sweep the red satin wisp from the line at the same time, before making his way slowly back to the safety of his flat.

Mr Johnston's hands trembled as he touched the garment again, holding it to his face and smoothing the fabric across his cheeks.

He had never felt like this before and was surprised at the rush of emotion that ensued. Surprised and, it must be admitted, delighted.

This was certainly the first time this had happened, but Mr Johnston was now determined that it wasn't going to be the last.

He might well be off to work in the morning wearing slightly damp clothes, but what was underneath would be more than worth the discomfort.

Mr Johnston decided that a whim was, after all, a very satisfying indulgence. He looked forward to seeing where it might lead in the future.

Stephanie a bubbly lady who has had an exciting life and now has settled down in Spain where she has joined the Writers Circle to improve her shrewd writing skills.

Speedy

S.J. Tarsus

Her heart was beating faster from the speed of the car. She glanced at him as they raced along, the reflection from the headlights shining on his rugged face.

'

Do you think, we will make it, Steve?' she asked him, her shaky voice betraying her worry.

'I am going as fast as I can' he said, while overtaking one of the few other cars on the road at that time of night. The other driver seemed irritated by his hasty manoeuvre and flashed his lights at them. Steve focused his eyes back on the road. 'But we still have about ten kilometres. Do you think you can hang in there?'

Mary tried to concentrate on her breathing as she had practiced in the prenatal course, but it seemed much harder now with the pain. It was their first baby and she wasn't due for another four weeks, but on this night, she had suddenly woken up and felt contractions. When her water broke, they both panicked a bit and rushed to the car.

'Try to calm your breathing and don't stress out' Steve suggested helpfully, when there was a sharp response from Mary.

'Telling me not to stress out, while I am trying hard not to stress out, isn't helping!' she exclaimed. The pain of the contractions made it hard to stay calm, but she tried to continue her rhythmic breathing.

Suddenly there was a noise and Steve almost lost control of the car. He hit the brakes and cursed. 'Bloody hell, not now!' With squealing tyres they came to a halt on the hard shoulder. He switched on the hazard warning lights, grabbed the high-vis jacket and opened the door to look at the car.
Mary saw him bending down at the left front and then he came back to the door. He sighed 'We have a flat tyre, I'll have to change it'.

He was about to turn away, but she grabbed his hand. 'Oh my god! How long is that going to take? I can't give birth in a car in the middle of nowhere!' Mary looked at him with panic in her eyes and felt the pain of the contractions worsening.

'Well, I haven't done it in a while, but I'll try to be... wait.... isn't that a car coming?'

Steve looked back and two headlights showed up on the road behind them. He quickly stepped onto the road, arms stretched out and waved at the approaching car.

The car stopped and the driver lowered his window. 'Hey, aren't you the ones, who just overtook me a few kilometres back? Not so fast now, hey?' He grinned a bit satisfied, but it faded quickly, when Steve started explaining their situation and the reason for speeding. 'Would it be too much to ask if you could drive us to the hospital? I could leave our car here and take care of it tomorrow.' Steve looked at the driver with pleading eyes.

The driver debated silently for a split second and then sighed 'Jeez, sure, hop in and let's go! I'm Jack by the way.'

'',,,,,

Last Orders

Richard Seal

Feeling weary at the prospect of another long week, landlord Mick sighed heavily as he slipped the bolts and opened the double doors of the small country pub at just after noon. Two of the elderly regulars, arriving dead on time as always, had already knocked on the doors a couple of times and shuffled glumly past him, mumbling under their breath about the landlord being five minutes late again. They watched him in sullen silence as he pulled the first of their customary three pints of mild, then they retired to sit in their usual corner, barely speaking to each other.

The Monday lunchtime session was not a particularly busy one, the pub's two rooms were occupied by the usual sprinkling of long-term regulars. There was one stranger present, however, and Mick was surprised to see him appearing to make a beeline for one particular seat. Despite being scrutinised disapprovingly by several of the old timers, the stranger with the inscrutable smile nursed his half a pint of bitter for a considerable period while sitting beneath the prominent 'Charlie's Corner' plaque on the wall.

As three o'clock approached and the lunchtime drinkers drifted away, the landlord was aware that the stranger was the last person remaining. As the man approached the bar, Mick was filled with a disconcerting inner chill. The figure was tall, gaunt and cadaverous, he was wearing a black coat with a hood which cast a shadow over a face which appeared to be somehow both grey and pale. The man fixed him with a blank yet penetrating stare before speaking in a low, guttural voice.

"I have come for Charlie .. " He paused, before adding. "When you see him this evening, I would be much obliged if you would tell him that I will be back to take him at last orders"

Mick could feel his stomach falling as the man spoke. Suddenly he found that he was sweating profusely, the man's heart had started racing and he could not hear anything other than the voice which seemed to permeate his being with inscrutable terror. He spoke tremulously:

"What do you mean?" He paused with uncertainty "Who are you, and where are you planning to take Charlie?"

"My name is Reaper. I have no doubt whatsoever that Charlie will remember me. I met him here in this room fifty years ago, and I told him the date and time when I would return."

"Fifty years ago! What on earth are you talking about? And what makes you think he will agree to go anywhere with you?" Mick was trying to sound confident and composed but was feeling overwhelmed by a dark sense of foreboding.

The man looked puzzled for a moment, before replying slowly. "There is no choice in this matter, Landlord - it is his time. He will leave here with me tonight"

Before Mick had the chance to say anything else, the man had slipped away into the shadows, disappearing into the heavy gloom of the November afternoon. Locking the doors behind him, the Landlord looked out into the windswept car park. He braced himself against the drizzle-laden breeze, but there was no sign of the man.

Mick felt unsettled and disorientated by his encounter with the stranger. These feelings remained with him over the next couple of hours as he finished clearing up then sat down to have lunch. He debated about whether he should speak to Charlie about the mysterious message when he came in as usual that evening, and if so, what would the man think? The Landlord began to think that he could have actually imagined the whole encounter - it had been a busy few weeks after all, he had been feeling under strain and off colour a lot lately. A fortnight's holiday was well overdue, but the brewery kept putting him off as they were struggling to find a relief to cover him.

Still feeling preoccupied when getting ready to open up again at five o'clock, Mick decided to check on the cellar first, as he had had several new barrels delivered that morning and they needed attention. No sooner had he walked down the steps than the door slammed shut. Puzzled and shocked, the Landlord rushed back up to the heavy door to find that it was stuck fast. How could it have blown shut? There were no windows open, and he was the only person on the premises ... Putting his shoulder to the door, Mick tried to force it open time and time again, but it almost felt like someone was pushing with all their strength in the other direction to keep him imprisoned. He could feel the sweat running down his back and sticking to his shirt and his heartbeat and sense of panic rising rapidly.

Finally, the door gave way to his pressure and he fell heavily onto the concrete floor at the top of the stairs. There was no one there, but the Landlord felt terrified, dazed and very close to losing consciousness. He lay there without moving for a couple of minutes, barely aware of his throbbing knee and grazed elbow, until his breathing had returned to something close to its normal rate.

When he got to his feet again and stumbled back into the bar, Mick could see that things were not right. The fittings, the decoration, the furniture and lighting ... everything around him looked different. The music on the jukebox was unmistakably from the nineteen fifties, and the customers looked different, yet somehow familiar. To a refrain of Elvis Presley singing 'Jailhouse Rock', He squinted, then rubbed his eyes in disbelief - it looked like many of the people were younger versions of the old men he saw in the bar every day. He could feel his insides starting to shrivel up within his body and wondered if he might be sick.

A young Jim Reynolds approached him and asked for a pint of bitter and one of his cheese and onion cobs "I hope it's fresher than the one I had yesterday," he grumbled.

Mick looked at him for a few moments without replying. "Jim? Is it you?"

The young man looked at him defensively, running his hand through thick blond hair which the Landlord assumed must have fallen out a long time ago. "Well, I'm Jim to some of my friends. You can call me James." Placing a few old pennies on the counter, he gave Mick a mirthless smile, took his sandwich and drink and returned to his seat. He looked back towards the bar a couple of times with an expression of bewilderment.

Mick looked down at the old money, then over at the ancient cash register. There were a few unappetising-looking ham and cheese cobs left in the transparent plastic box on the counter, just like his grandfather had described to him, with a nostalgic grin, many years ago. Nearby there was also a large jar of what he assumed to be pickled eggs, and a smaller one of onions. There was no sign of the credit card machine, no-one was glued to their mobile phone and virtually everyone in both rooms appeared to be smoking.

The Landlord stopped in his tracks when he saw the unmistakable figure of a very much younger and almost fresh-faced looking Charlie Miller sitting in his corner, playing dominoes with friends. He was not wearing his ever-present flat cap, and he was smoking a cigarette instead of his trademark pipe, but he was drinking his usual pint of bitter with a whisky chaser and his heavy-set features and truculent expression were unmistakable.

Suddenly the bar doors opened and the distinctive figure of Reaper, looking exactly the same as when Mick had seen him that lunchtime, walked in purposefully and headed straight for Charlie. Instinctively, he dashed out from behind the bar and seized him before he had a chance to reach his target or say anything to him. The Landlord told the bemused - looking customer to stay back and bundled Reaper out of the pub, but in the process there was a scuffle and Mick received a heavy blow to the face. Before he blacked out, he heard the eerie voice say "I will be back to collect ..."

Finding himself lying on the floor beside the bar door, the Landlord opened his eyes slowly, and focused on the several gnarled faces looking down at him. The men were too feeble to haul the sturdy man back to his feet, but for a few moments they seemed to be almost as concerned about him as they were about the delay in having their evening drinks served up.

"What have you been up to, Mick? Drinking your own profits?"

"Lying down on the job again, you just can't get the staff these days!"

"It's a bit cold for sunbathing, Gaffer! Can't you wait for your annual trip to the Bahamas?"

Mick's heart skipped a beat when he saw old Jim. He grabbed him by the arm "Seriously, Jim, what happened?"

The man looked at him gravely. "You opened the doors then just seemed to collapse on the spot, pass out. How are you feeling now?"

"I'm OK, I think, I just feel a bit confused .. " His head was thumping.

"Are you quite sure? You don't need us to call a doctor?"

"No, thanks." He rubbed his face slowly, then shook his head a couple of times in a vain attempt to clear his thoughts.

"In that case ... " a different voice chimed in " .. Let's get the show on the road. I'm gasping for a pint!"

Smiling now, he walked back into the present-day version of the pub with the men and started pouring their beers. After a busy evening during which he had indulged in a few drinks himself, had a few laughs and got involved in a lot of banter and teasing, Mick was just starting to feel normal again. He was a little puzzled that many of the regulars had not been in that night, and something still felt a bit different about the pub somehow, but he could not put his finger on what it was.

He was about to ring the final bell at eleven o'clock when he looked up to see the shadowy Reaper standing in front of him. His thin lips were twisted into a grim smile.

"Good evening."

Mick felt the colour draining from his cheeks. "I haven't seen Charlie, he hasn't been in tonight"

The stranger shook his head slowly. "No, of course he hasn't. The man died of throat cancer ten years ago." He paused, frowning. "He hasn't been in here for a long time. Perhaps you haven't noticed that he doesn't have a plaque."

Mick could see that there was still a plaque in Charlie's corner, but it looked different and he could not read it from this distance. "What are you saying .. ?"

The stranger fixed the cold gaze on the Landlord again. "Jim Reynolds received that accolade a few years ago. He doesn't look particularly grateful to have a corner named after him though, does he?" He cleared his throat before speaking again. "I hope I didn't hurt you with that punch, that's quite a black eye you've got there!"

Mick felt his face gingerly. "I'm fine, no thanks to you! So why have you come in here again then?" He tried to mask his fear with heavy sarcasm. "Aren't you tempted to take your brand of wit and wisdom down the road to the Anchor? They have a Happy Hour on Mondays .."

"Why am I here?" The stranger's expression had turned malevolent, and his eyes were black. "It should have been Charlie Miller's time to go now, but you are responsible for changing that, aren't you? All this is down to you. I told you I would be back to collect."

"Collect? Collect what?"

Reaper placed a bony hand firmly on Mick's shoulder. "It's last orders, Landlord ... "

""""

The Bodega in Hondon de las Nieves

The opening chapter from Percy's

Death for a Starter

which won the Pinnacle Award for
best historical fiction.
The story developed into a trilogy
with two further novels 'The
Dauntless Factor' and 'The Cormack's'

Chapter One

Middle of the eighteen hundred's, Ireland.
The O'Dowd's Small Holding

Alicia was desperate as she searched for food for her two children, Patrick and Florence. The ground was wet and very muddy. Her feet were icy, in shoes which were badly worn, giving little protection against the bitter cold. She was digging with her bare hands and holding a medium size sharp pointed knife to help in moving the soil to one side, trying to find a potato that had survived the blight. With a heavy heart she could see the fungus had spread across the plot of land, and that the leaves had wilted turning to a dirty looking brown with round blackish spots. Although knowing it was useless, with her husband and son, both of whom were on other areas of the patch of ground, continuing their search for just one of the vegetables which had survived the disease.

She was feeling very tired, as it was almost a week since Alicia had eaten a fulfilling meal and the lack of proper food was starting to tell on her health. She looked up and her heart missed a beat as Reuben was holding up something, and in that moment, Alicia knew he had found one that had survived the infection.

It had started to rain in a soft drizzle, like a heavy mist, as he started to make his way towards her. Tears flooded her eyes as she looked at the man she loved, and saw what the years, this terrible food shortage and constant worry had done to him. When they had married ten years previously, they had so much hope. She had expected to continue the life she had had with her parents, living in luxury without having to work. In those days he was a strong man who stood tall – right now as he staggered across the field he was stooped, dressed in rags with mud over his legs and arms, looking far older than his years.

The hope vanished from her when she saw what he had in his hand. Although a full-size potato she knew in her heart as soon as they cut into it the flesh would be inedible. Large tears ran down her cheeks as she flung her arms around him and cried on his shoulder. The rain adding to their depression as the cold water fell on each head and ran down the back of their necks.

"Mather" - it was their son Patrick. He like them had been working on another part of the small holding and he was calling beside the little cottage they called home. The stone-built structure with its thatched roof was not very secure against the weather, a small building like so many others that had been built across the Irish countryside. Inside were just two tiny rooms where they lived, straw mattresses on the floor at night and during the day rickety wooden furniture littered the rooms for comfort of the barest minimum. In one corner was a small fireplace, which was rarely lit, as they could not afford to buy the fuel for it, and what kindling they could find in the fields surrounding them, was too wet to light for the warmth of a fire.

From the far side of their home she could see a well-dressed man on a black horse which was travelling down the narrow path. She knew at once it was the Land Agent, the man responsible for collecting rent and to do the bidding of the English Landlord. But this was a person she did not recognise. She turned and looked at her husband, "Who is he? What do you think he wants?"

"It has to be somebody about the rent and no doubt to check on the growth of their hay." Because they could not afford to pay rent the Landlord had allowed them to supply him with produce, which they had to grow from their own resources.

"But the growth has been so poor because of the foul weather - also I can't help feeling that the potato blight has something to do with it. What can we do?" Alicia was frightened and knew this was not going to be good news.

A rare smile crossed his lips, "We have got nothing more to offer them." He took hold of her hand as they turned to struggle in the mud to the cottage.

The agent was a burly man who was smartly dressed in shiny boots and a leather jacket. He was holding a sword at his side as he dismounted from the horse, a completely black mare.

Once on the ground, he looked at them in distaste and turning, he took a board out of the pannier strapped to the horse behind the saddle. He looked at the paper attached to the board. "You have some land where your kind landlord has allowed you to grow hay instead of paying him rent. I need to see it, where is it?"

Reuben was shaking his head, "The seeds need some warmth for it to grow, it will look better when the weather changes." He had started to walk to one side of the cottage.

The agent was not pleased with what he saw, "Is this all?"

"Yes. When our farm was taken from us and we were told to farm this...(he waved his hands at the plot)...but the ground is too poor to grow crops on..." He wanted to shout at the man but knew it would be useless and would not help, instead his voice sounded weary and without conviction.

The agent turned and slapped him across the face. "How dare you, you ungrateful people. That grass had better recover very soon and be ready for the scythe." He then walked quickly to another part of their ground.

Alicia could feel the temper building inside her as she followed, the knife still in her right hand tucked out of sight up the rags of a sleeve.

"As you are not producing enough to pay the rent, this area will need to be turned into hay." He was pointing to a small plot on which a small skinny cow was grazing, the animal supplied the family with enough milk for them so they could survive.

"But that is not possible. Where would the animal go? There is no other place." Alicia was nodding her head as she listened to her husband.

"That is not our problem. You entered into an agreement, now stick to it." He turned to walk back to the horse, tucking the board under his arm, pushing Reuben out of the way as he did so. Reuben muttered "Forced into an agreement more like!"

Alicia moved and stood in front of him, "I suppose it does not matter to you if we die of starvation, as my Mother and Father did last year. All you want is our food and to leave us with nothing." She was talking slowly with tears running down her cheeks. She could not remember being so angry and furious at what this man was saying. She also knew, like so many others they would not be able to continue to exist, which they were barely doing now. Without the feeble milk they were getting from the cow they would have nothing, and her children would suffer. It flashed through her mind - in that case why should he not suffer as well?

She stood her ground as he moved forward. She could hear her husband telling her to move out of his way. She shouted at the agent, "How do I feed the bairns? Eh! Go on tell me."

He was looking down at her grinning, "That is nothing to do with me," before he could say anything more she swung her right hand upwards. The knife, which she had been holding in her fist, with the blade held along her wrist could not be seen under the pieces of cloth she was wearing. Suddenly she reversed it, the blade flashed as she forced it upwards. There was a hesitation as it tried to penetrate the leather of the jacket. Using more vigour, the knife continued, the sharp pointed end went easily into him and continued up under his ribs.

There was no noise, just blood gushing out over the blade and her hand. With a surprised look on his face the agent silently dropped to the ground. Reuben looked at her astounded wondering what had happened; she was still standing and looking down in shock. She watched as Patrick pulled the blade from the visitor's chest, blood covering his hand and more on the rags he was wearing.

The agent lying on the ground had not moved. The couple standing beside the body were looking at each other, both wondering how it had happened whilst knowing they were in deep trouble.

There was a scream - Florence, their daughter had come out of the shack and was standing near them shivering and starting to cry. Her mother took her in her arms rocking her and whilst still looking at her husband, her mind was in a whirl, knowing if and when the authorities found out they would all be hanged for murder.

Alicia in her heart knew what she had done was wicked, but what the man had intended was equally so, condemning a family to die from starvation like many others in that terrible time for Ireland. They both knew that now they had a death on their hands they would have to make a new start.

ωπππ

The Hondon Valley

Gardener

Richard Seal

When the Harrison family moved into the cavernous house on the hill, they quickly embarked upon an extensive modernisation programme. The kitchen and bathrooms were gutted, the entire interior was redecorated, sash windows were ripped out in favour of modern UPVC, and a conservatory was added. Father was very pleased with his new car port, while Mother insisted on gravel replacing the patchy grass and pesky weeds. She bought a few pots so that she could select a few easy-to-manage plants to add some colour to the patio and barbecue area.

Twelve-year-old Marcus and his ten year old sister Simone were encouraged to go round to their friends' houses rather than bringing them home, as their parents were not keen on either the house or garden being messed up. The children were more than happy with this policy as neither of them fancied the idea of playing on the gravel surface anyway. One Saturday afternoon the siblings were wandering together at the very end of the plot when they noticed that there was a small gap in the thick privet hedge, on the right-hand side.

Marcus poked his head through the space. "Wow, you should see the garden next door - it's like a forest, really wild-looking and overgrown."

"Let me have a look." The sight caused the girl's eyes to widen. "It looks so exciting, there are so many trees. You could play hide and seek in there all day."

"Come on, let's go in and have a little look around."

"Should we? Won't the people be angry if they see us?" Her face crinkled with a deep frown.

"Don't worry, Simone, it will be fine. I will just say that I'm looking for a lost football."

"I don't know ... " However, the girl had no choice in the matter as her brother propelled her through the space ahead of him.

The garden was delightfully untamed and atmospheric. The ancient trees were twisted and gnarled, their roots creeping back up through the earth to point like accusing fingers, unkempt bushes had taken on new identities and encroached onto the moss-covered paths, while butterflies and bees criss-crossed the summer air as they came and went between a range of wild flowers.

"I love it here," Simone whispered, "I bet there are fairies somewhere."

"Snakes too, maybe," he grinned. "I wouldn't be surprised to see some extinct animals too."

Suddenly the children spotted a small house up ahead. It was quite difficult to distinguish between the building and the oak trees which almost seemed to be part of the fabric of the walls. A chocolate Labrador came over to greet them, he did not bark but licked their hands and panted excitedly. His tail was wagging ten to the dozen.

"What a lovely dog," Simone was already on her knees, stroking him softly. "I wish Mum and Dad would let us have one."

"They don't like any animals really do they? It's a shame." He put his hand on the dog's head, which caused his tail to move even faster. "Good boy."

They tentatively approached the house and found that the front door was ajar. There was no one inside. However, the dog led them round to the other side of the property where an old man was in the process of planting something. He was smiling, but totally absorbed in what he was doing and did not look up for several moments.

"Hello, my dears, I get lost in my gardening and don't want to be found sometimes. How nice to meet you." The man gave them a broad smile.

"Sorry, I hope you don't mind us being here ... " Marcus began to apologise, before the man stopped him.

"Please, be my guests. Come inside and let me make you both some tea."

After introductions they went in and had a long chat with Vincent, in the company of his thirteen-year-old dog, Willow. To her delight, Simone found that the wooden chairs that they were sitting on were curiously misshapen and irregular, and the table and other objects in the kitchen looked the same. The man explained that he had been living there for most of his life, and he had retired from his job as a gardener five years ago, just after his wife had died.

"I don't manage to keep the garden in order, I'm afraid." He paused, and his deep blue eyes twinkled as he looked at them. "Not because it's too much work, I prefer nature to find its own way and I'm happy to follow its lead."

"Your garden has got such an amazing feeling," Simone said excitedly. "You and your flowers seem to get on so well together."

"Thank you, they are the best friends you could have. All you need to do is show them love and kindness and they will respond." The man had a faraway look in his eyes. "We have no grass or flowers, nothing grows in our garden really," Marcus added, "Mum puts a few plants in pots now and again, but they never seem to survive. I think she forgets to water them."

The man looked at the boy with an expression of deep sorrow. "Plants need care, and they love to feel the earth beneath their stems, to stretch their roots out around the worms before they can secure their own special place in the sun. It makes them feel complete."

"Do you grow vegetables too?" Simone looked around to see if she could spot any.

"Yes, I will show you my allotment area. At the moment I am planting carrots and radishes. Oh and some cauliflowers too - they are wonderful cool weather vegetables you know, particularly delicious when roasted."

The children were so entranced that they asked him if they could return the following day so see some more. "Of course, you are welcome anytime, I'll give you a guided tour and introduce you to my favourite shrubberies."

Over the next few weeks, Marcus and Simone often slipped next door to chat to the man, to play in the garden and explore its nooks and crannies, or to watch him at work planting snowdrops, bluebells, daffodils, tulips, crocuses and anemones. Vincent taught the children so much about flowers and vegetables, and their parents commented that the tomatoes he gave them were so big and tasted better than the organic ones that they bought from the supermarket.

Marcus was intrigued that he never wore gloves for protection. "Don't your hands get scratched and cut, Vincent?"

"Marcus, I prefer to feel the soil on my fingers, I want to feel as close as possible to the creative source. I don't really like pesticides either - insects have their rightful place in the ecosystem too."

As the summer holiday began to draw to a close, mother took Marcus and Simone aside one morning. She told them that the hedges were being removed and replaced by fences the following week as they were easier for father to maintain. There would no longer be a gap in the boundary for the children to creep through.

When the youngsters approached Vincent that afternoon, he looked even more blissfully content amongst his flower beds than usual, which helped them to feel a bit less sad as they explained the situation to him.

"Children, let me give you some cuttings to take away. Look after these beauties and they will reward you."

"Thank you, Vincent, we hope we will see you again," Marcus said, sadly.

"Yes, we will miss you so much." Simone started to cry.

"I will still be here, my dears, there's no need to worry. I'm not far away." The man tried to reassure them.

Long after the fences had been installed, the children continued to tend to their small patch of lavender and geraniums in a peaceful, distant corner of their garden. Occasionally there was a rustling of foliage near the boundary, and the siblings took comfort in the distinctive sound of Vincent whistling to himself.

""""

Ayuntamiento de Hondón de los Frailes

This extract
from the exciting novel
White Gold

by Trudie Le Beau
Is set in the seventeen hundred's ...
the book is available through Amazon and book
stores through its ISBN 978-0-9955729-5-9

.

PROLOGUE

MAY 1789

Christy Duggan hauled on his oar as he and his fellow crewmen rowed out to The Elizabeth with the last of the stores needed for their impending voyage. He looked down at his well-honed muscles flexing and relaxing under his sweat moistened skin as the oar moved back and forth. He was a sturdily built young man with a physique that many would envy and a face that though not strikingly handsome, was nonetheless pleasant and even featured. He was a newcomer to the existing crew on the Elizabeth and to all intents and purposes was every inch the affable, accommodating recruit that he purported to be, his external appearance giving no clue that on the inside he was a poison filled vessel with a soul as black as Hades; a cruel and twisted being with nothing but hate in his heart.

He had tracked down Jake Faraday and his runt of a companion with just one aim, to kill them. To make them suffer as he had done since they had slaughtered his lover Charlie.   Since Charlie's death he had been haunted by the sight that had met him that dreadful day in a seedy lodging house in Calais where his lover had met his end, throat slit and kneeling in a pool of blood in a parody of prayer.   He had to admit to himself that he had been a little jealous when Charlie had refused his offer to help dispatch the runt, resenting the obsession he seemed to have for the boy. If only he had insisted on going along Charlie would still be alive and those two bastards would be dead – no doubt about it.   *"Oh Charlie, if only, if only!"*

He strained pulling against the white capped waves that seemed determined to push the small craft back to shore, but the grimace on his face was not from effort, his face was contorted with hatred as he looked back at the party still on the jetty saying their last farewells.

Lizzie and John Faraday hugged their son Jake and his best friend India whom they had come to love as their own; all four of them trying to quell the tears that were threatening to engulf them.   "Come on Ma, we'll be back before you know it.   It's just a straightforward trip to the islands and then on to visit George, Beau and the others to see how they've settled in Jamaica. We'll be gone less than a year and with all that's going on at Spinnaker I bet you won't even miss us."

Lizzie held her son's face in her hands.   "You promise me son, you'll stay away from any trouble and," turning to India and pinching his cheek, "that you'll bring this rascal back in one piece. Promise me now or you'll not be going."

Jake picked his mother up and swung her round. "How can we possibly stay away for long?   There's no-one can cook like you Ma and I'm missing your meat pie and dumplings already."

Lizzie blushed "Oh, you silly young 'un, I'm being serious!"

Jake turned to his Pa. "I'm glad Eli is staying with you Pa. You've got so many things to see to so don't forget now, any extra help, anything you need, just get it. I've made provision for you to have all the money you may need so don't go trying to do everything yourself, not with you having been so ill and all. I'm really looking forward to seeing your new workshop being finished when I get back, so you'd better get a shift on!"

John put an arm round both men - they were boys no longer, both extremely handsome but very different. Jake was tall, strong and tanned with a broad chest, long strong legs and a thick head of chestnut hair that was tied at the nape of his neck. India was almost the same height with a lighter but well-muscled frame. His olive skin and short glossy black hair portraying that he did not share his ancestry with his adopted family. "Get off with you then, and Jake try to put Alice and all that has happened from your mind. None of those damned Villiers are worth a second thought, you're ten times better than them – we all are." Seeing the pain in his son's eyes he regretted his last words as soon as he had uttered them. He squeezed Jake hard. "Just do like your Ma says and stay out of trouble!"

Jake and Indy climbed into the last dinghy to leave the jetty, both taking an oar, unable to see their loved ones clearly through tear filled eyes.

"'""'""

The founder member and the driving force for the development of the Writers Circle was

Lin Penhaul

The following is memories of a time on the beach.

LATE AFTERNOON

"Heaven is a sandy beach with room to sunbathe"
That's what my city dwelling friends tell me, but as I walked I saw things differently. The late afternoon sun felt warm on my face and the slight breeze brought a salty tang to my tongue.

I could tell without looking that the tide was about half-way out. Neither the thrusting slap of high tide nor the pebble-dragging grind of low tide could be heard, only the gentle ripple of the slack.

Little whorls on the damp sand told of lugworms trying to hide from the early morning bait –diggers. Curving lines of pebbles dredged from the ocean, smoothly contoured in witness to the harsh passage marked the tide line, their browns, creams and pearly whites dulling as they dried.
Still pools under slimy green rocks provided home for tiny soft-shelled crabs scurrying out of sight as any threatening shadow appeared on the water.

Overhead gulls swooped and cried, cutting the sky into segments then landing to bob up and down like little paper boats on a pond.

Frantic sanderlings made punctured patterns on the sandy ridges, rushing hither and thither seemingly without purpose whilst the stolid turnstones got on with the job of grubbing for sand - hoppers.

The oystercatchers, wading in the surf tried to call them to order with his sharp pill-pill but even his striking black and white plumage and orange beak could not distract them.
Certainly, there was no shortage of food as the empty shells around testified. Black mussel shells with pearly linings lay side by side with delicate pink tellinas. Sharp edged razors, fan scallops and blue-tinged nutshells were empty houses; debris in the glistening tangle of bladder wrack by the water's edge.

Higher up the beach where the dunes began, low prickly Saltwort was interspersed with the pink and gold of Herb Robert and Knapweed. Scarlet Pimpernel winked his eye cheerfully, but the handsome black and yellow cinnabar caterpillars chewed unheeding as if conscious that only their diligent feeding could control the rampant ragwort.

I turned for a last glance, to see a skein of knots pulling the dusk like a final curtain across the horizon, folding the day softly into night.

""""

A government big enough to give you everything you want, is strong enough to take everything you have.
Thomas Jefferson

It has been rewarding for the group to see Tarika, who is Scandinavian, develop her second language of English.

This piece by Tarika seems suitable to end Story Telling Twenty Seven.

Bye my Beloved

Janne Tarika Gravdal

Loving someone is easy when everything is new and exciting. But what happens and why does it happen? Well! I do not know. But we are two different people and it takes a lot to make a relationship sustaining and to maintain each other's needs and wishes at all times over the years.

In a relationship there will always be turbulent years of good and bad times, but the art is to listen to each other, be there for each other in every situation. But when it's no longer possible, it's time to say goodbye and let go of the one you love and let them and yourself move on in life. So goodbye my beloved and happiness for the future.

Percychatteybooks

Story Telling (R)

Somerset House

6070 Birmingham Business Park

Birmingham

B37 7BF

Registered Number 2299335

All of Percy Chattey Books and Story Telling, are available
from Amazon and other outlets.
(00 34) 603 472 476

www.ingramcontent.com/pod-product-compliance
Lightning Source LLC
Chambersburg PA
CBHW060628130626
46555CB00002B/713